FOREVER WICKED

WICKED #4

PIPER LAWSON

Line and copy editing by Cassie Roberston and Joy Editing
Cover by Natasha Snow
Cover photography by Lindee Robinson

1

HALEY

FIVE DAYS UNTIL THE WEDDING

There's nothing like a man on his knees.

Naked to the waist, eyes closed.

Especially when that man is Jax Jamieson and he's on his knees for me.

"I wonder if you taste as good as I remember."

The biggest rock star in a generation yanks my skirt up around my hips, his half-lidded eyes locking on their target between my thighs.

My greedy gaze roams his gorgeous face

and tight jaw, his sculpted shoulders and chest and abs.

It still blows my mind that he's mine.

The damp air in the garage is nothing compared to the dampness between my legs right now.

"It hasn't been that long," I protest breathily, my hands kneading his shoulders.

"No man should be without his wife for a month before their wedding."

"It's not fair to him?"

"It's not fair to her."

Our plan to sell my father's house in Philadelphia before moving the last of my, and his, belongings to Jax's mansion in Dallas with time to spare before the wedding had seemed foolproof.

Still, some emergency roadblocks complicated the sale, meaning I'd had to spend the last month in Philly while Jax and Annie were here in Dallas because of Annie's school and a promotional gig Jax had committed to.

Now with less than a week until the wedding, we're still tripping over moving boxes from Philly while our friends and loved ones are descending on Dallas.

Did I mention we haven't gotten a moment alone together since I got back?

Jax's hands skim up my thighs, thumbs grazing so close to where I need him.

"Wider." That voice the world has paid millions to hear is commanding, and right now, it's commanding me.

My body tries to comply, desperate to give him access to what he wants—what we want—but my foot is blocked by something hard.

I try to lift my leg higher, to catch the top of the cardboard moving box, but there's another stacked on top of it and my foot slides back down.

On a growl, Jax grabs my hips and turns me without even rising. My shoulder blades hit a metal shelf, and I suck in a breath, but I manage to widen my stance a few inches.

Each pore on my body, each fiber of my being, insists that Jax's tongue between my thighs will fix every ache I own.

He's hovering millimeters from where I need him. Vibration tingles through my body, radiating down my legs, to my fingertips that grab his shoulders for balance. The muscles there ripple, making the tattoos down his bicep and forearm jump in time to my heartbeat.

"Tell me how much you missed me," he rasps.

I take a moment to appreciate Jax's fiery amber eyes, the cocky tilt of his full mouth, the determined line of his jaw.

"I might have thought of you once or twice," I say saucily because I take my job of managing his enormous ego seriously. "I also thought about seating charts and flowers and whether we should add a sorbet to dessert."

He hooks a finger in the panel of my panties, already soaked, and drags it to the side. His breath on me has me trembling.

Though I hadn't been looking forward to spending time away from Jax, I'd reasoned it would be possible. I spent twenty-one years without him; a few weeks wouldn't kill me.

Apparently, that was optimistic. Because in those twenty-one years, I hadn't gotten used to his commanding presence at my side and in my bed like I have in the year we've been engaged.

It was like growing up without the sun only

to be forced back underground the moment you experienced its warmth.

During my month alone in Philly, I learned phone sex does less to resolve tension than to escalate it. And getting myself off to the memory of my fiancé's touch, his lips, his cock, is a poor substitute for the real thing.

"The only dessert you thought of is me eating this pussy until you're begging me to stop."

His finger slides against my entrance. *Not fair.*

He teases me until I moan.

"Yes," I whisper.

But instead of devouring me like I want him to, Jax pulls back.

"We're going upstairs." His breath is unsteady. "I'm going to lock the door. And fuck my future wife until she swears to never leave me again."

His words have me boneless, but even though I want to float away on a wave of desire, the logical part of my brain won't leave.

"I can't take this afternoon off," I manage. "I have a dress appointment, then I need to find somewhere quiet to review an app for Carter and... oh—"

Jax's finger flicks my clit hard enough that I jump.

"Don't say his name when I'm fucking you." His harsh edge is dulled by the wave of pleasure radiating from my core as his fingers continue to caress my opening.

"You're not fucking me. You're teasing me." My hands flex in his hair as need to assert myself twines with longing, the ever-present temptation to ignore the world and say yes to anything this man could ask of me. "And I can't drop work for this entire week on account of the wedding."

"I don't want you to drop work for a week. I want you to drop it for two."

His fingers press inside me as if to prove a point, and this time, I do moan. It's impossible to reconcile the sudden fullness in me with the need for more as my hips arch against his hand.

"Next week it'll be you and me on a beach in Bali, and every sweet inch of this"—his thumb rubs a circle over my clit, and I hiccup at the bolt of desire that shocks me—"is mine until I say so."

Bali. It's like a prayer. Something to cling to when it's all too much.

Sand.

Solitude.

Me and the man I love and zero interruptions.

I'd figured once everything in Philly was finalized and my belongings were here, the actual wedding would be straightforward, but since the moment invitations went out more than six months ago, congratulations and gifts have poured in by the hundreds.

The biggest wedding of the decade—which has nothing to do with me and everything to do with the fact that I'm marrying Jax Jamieson—has gone from "massive" to "Richter scale registering," a storm that's built its own velocity and is threatening to destroy everything in its path.

But Jax's mouth lowers between my thighs, and I know the desperate ache in me is about to resolve.

"Promise you're mine for the next two weeks," he murmurs against my needy skin, "and I'll make you come so hard they'll hear you back in Philly."

The vibration from Jax's mouth has me clutching the shelf behind me, fingers slipping on the cold metal as I swallow a moan. But the feel of his soft hair in my fingers, his hot mouth between my thighs, his commanding grip on my ass, tears at my control. "*Yes.*"

"Fuck, I love hearing you say that word. Almost makes up for all the times you told me no."

White-hot pleasure descends on me as his mouth finally claims me.

My fingers grasp for the shelf, and this time it tips forward—just a few inches, but enough to send something rolling off the front.

"Jax, look out!" I startle out of my haze fast enough grab the can of paint as it drops through the air, a millisecond before it lands on his beautiful face.

The shock of what nearly happened rips through the arousal, leaving me shaking with adrenaline.

My almost-husband smirks. "We're not even married yet, and you're trying to kill me?"

I set the can on the floor, shaking off the

horror from the sight of it falling toward Jax. "I don't want to kill you," I pant. "I'd miss your mouth too much."

Jax straightens, eyes glowing as he brushes an impatient thumb down my cheek. "I miss every part of you, Hales, and we're both right here."

My heart melts as I take in the man I love, the one I still can't believe I'm marrying in a few days.

His dirty words have me aching again. He trails a finger down my stomach, making my breath hitch before it dips between my thighs.

"Haley! Jax! I know what you're doing in there," a voice shouts through the closed door to the house.

I squeeze my eyes shut as Jax's hand stills, willing us both to block out the sound.

When nothing comes after one heartbeat, two, five, I think I've succeeded.

Until a pounding comes at the door.

"Haley, you have a dress fitting in thirty minutes, and there's an accident in town! We need to leave now."

Alarm breaks through my sex-induced

haze. "Shit! I thought it wasn't for another hour and a half."

"I won't be done with you in thirty minutes. But if they want to come to the house, I can work under the dress."

My thighs press together at his seductive promise.

"I'm coming in," Serena threatens, separated from us by only a few inches of wood.

My face drains of blood.

"Fucking hell." Jax withdraws from my body, and I bite my lip to stop from complaining. He starts toward the door, fury in every taut muscle.

"Jax! Stop it." I lunge, hooking two fingers in the waist of his jeans and wincing as they nearly dislocate. I manage to get between him and the door without tripping over myself, and I work my clothes back into place between words. "Don't bite Serena's head off. It's not her fault."

Frustration and concern color the amber eyes I love. "Let's elope. I'll have a charter on the tarmac in an hour."

My lips curve into a trembling smile. "We

wanted to do this right, remember? I wanted our friends. You wanted it in Dallas..."

Reluctant hands help me straighten my ruined underwear and wrinkled skirt as he drops his forehead to mine.

"Fine, but I'm going to make you come once for every night we spent apart," he vows. "You're getting at least a week of orgasms tonight."

He presses his mouth to mine in a hard kiss that's a reminder of what we were just doing and that the patience he's exhibiting right now is a gift.

"What're you doing this afternoon?" I ask. "Helping Brick taste-test the cake? Or arranging carbon offsets for all the guests with Kyle?"

"Something better." His eyes gleam as if he's holding a secret over my head simply to punish me.

It's working.

I'm dying to know, but hearing my name shouted through the door again pulls my attention away.

"This isn't over. Tonight." He presses my

hand against the bulge in his jeans that has me lusting after him even more.

With a last look that does nothing to cool my insides, he grabs his shirt off the floor, tugs it over his head, and starts for the door.

2

HALEY

"You look hot. I'm seriously attracted to you right now."

I laugh as I trace the lines of my dress, meeting Serena's playful gaze in the mirror at the boutique. "Remember Wes? Your seriously attractive genius of a boyfriend?"

My friend waves and goes back to working the zipper up the back of my dress. With her pale-purple floor-length gown, her blond ponytail, and her trademark red lipstick, she looks like one badass maid of honor. "If he was going to lose me, he'd respect that it was to a fellow nerd."

I bite my cheek. I love seeing my friend happy.

Every one of the handful of times I met Serena's boyfriend over the past year, I wished I got more time with him. The guy has a PhD in genetics and started a DNA dating app that's slowly taking over the world.

He also melts when he looks at Serena. My friend is a marketing ninja who can plan parties and deal with egos without breaking a sweat. They're opposites, but they're also so cute it hurts to watch them together.

"You guys moved in together this year, but you've been strangely quiet about how it's going."

"Only because we've been busy christening every surface of the new apartment." Her lips curve. "But I like where we're at. This 'we're serious but not ready to require lawyers in order to fight over the potted fig tree in the living room' place."

I laugh. "Well, I hope he understands what he's getting into by spending the week here."

"He's level-headed like you," Serena insists, screwing up her face. "The craziness won't even make a dent. How's Jax handling it?"

"He's been edgy since before I went to Philly," I admit. "Big Leap was denied national funding that would've expanded the music program to new states, and I think he took it personally."

"Where is Big Leap? I didn't see it in the driveway."

I think of the renovated tour bus turned mobile studio we use to run music workshops for underprivileged kids.

"In Philly with staff for the summer. Jax will go back to it eventually, but he's not used to rejection. When we got the bad news, he decided to fund its expansion himself. I told him that defeats the purpose of having partners. We need to collaborate."

"And?"

"And he did it anyway." I roll my eyes, though I can't deny his heart's in the right place. The money he invested will help staff take the bus to two new states over the summer, linking up with local community outreach programs, but our ultimate goal is to integrate with elementary and high schools.

"I think he knows that to expand in the long run, we need to play within the rules. But red tape to Jax is like a red cape to a bull—all he sees is a signal to charge.

"In the meantime, he says he's been doing things around the house, but whenever I try to talk to him about his future, he tells me not to 'deny a man his hard-earned retirement'."

Serena snorts. "Jax will never retire."

I think she's right, but Jax is the last person to admit it.

My friend looks back at the dress. "Okay, suck in a second. I'm going to get this fastened if it kills me."

I do, and Serena shoves the zipper up with a cry of triumph.

I take as much of a breath as I can manage given the tight fabric. "Listen," I gasp, "I appreciate you taking charge on the dresses and the bachelorette."

Serena waves me off. "Nina's doing the hard work."

Since Jax's former tour manager started dating Brick after years of flirtation, she's been stepping away from life on the road and into local event planning.

This wedding was the perfect opportunity. She knows Jax and the circus that follows him better than anyone.

"Must feel like old times," Serena prompts.

"It does. Except Lita couldn't make it because she's touring. But Jerry's flying in tomorrow."

"How is he?"

I chew my lip. "I visited him last week. The medication has done wonders to help him stabilize over the past year. Still, you can slow Alzheimer's, but you can't stop it."

"I'm sorry you couldn't get him to move here."

I nod tightly. "It's his decision, and I understand it."

But I had hoped to move Jerry, the man who took me under his wing on Jax's tour, to a facility near us in Dallas. I'd researched options, found the best possible care. But when I presented it to him, he rejected the idea outright.

It'd never occurred to me that, without any family to speak of, he might choose to stay in Philly. Even though Jax and I have committed to visiting Jerry every chance we get, Jerry's decision is a reminder that I'm leaving behind the only home I've known.

New beginnings don't come without endings.

"He's going to be so proud of you this weekend. Your mom would be, too."

Serena's words bring me back, and I find a smile. "I miss her." I know she, like my father, had a hand in bringing me and Jax together. I know they'd both be happy in their own way if they hadn't passed. "But I'm glad you're here."

Serena squeezes my hand.

"You ladies decent?" The designer walks in without waiting for an answer.

The petite woman who can't be much older than us cocks her head, yanking a pencil from the messy chestnut bun pinned on top. "Don't worry. I've seen a lot over the years. Nothing under there"—she waves her pencil at us—"could shock me."

Serena and I picked out a dress last year, but when I saw Ava Cameron's designs, I changed my mind. This dress is my one "rock star's wife" indulgence, even though I insisted on paying for it myself.

It turns out the woman is even more amazing than the clothing she dreams up.

"Thank you for flying in from New York to do last-minute adjustments," I say, fluffing my skirt. "Do you do this for all your clients?"

Ava flashes a broad smile as she bends to inspect the hemline. "Hell no. But when you called me, you seemed overwhelmed." Her competent hands fly over the lace. "I can't help with the cake or the man, but the dress?" Her green eyes flash. "I can always take care of the dress."

She straightens. "What are you doing for shoes?"

I lift the skirt to reveal the kitten heels I brought in my purse.

"Perfect. And are you doing the old, new, borrowed, and blue thing?"

I cock my head. "Honestly, I hadn't much thought about it. Blue doesn't go with the bridesmaid dresses."

"Agreed. Screw tradition. You do you." She makes a few notes on her clipboard. "So Nina has already come in for final fittings. Yours is done, Serena. We're just waiting for Annie."

"Her aunt Grace should be here with her soon," I say. "They just arrived back from an end-of-school-year trip to France."

Ava makes a little groan as she moves to my waist. "I love France. My man Nate's been promising to take me for months now."

"Sounds romantic. Maybe the next dress you make will be for yourself," Serena teases.

"I'm not making my own wedding dress. Screw that. I'll make my girls design it for me," she decides as she works.

"Are they designers?"

"Hell no. Lex and Jordan are my business partners. But it'd be worth it to see their faces when I ask them."

Her full mouth purses as she pinches the fabric at my waist. "So, what are your plans for the week nutritionally? Are you a juicer? Because I'd give these Manolos for a quarter to a half an inch on this."

I smooth a hand down my stomach. "Oh. No, I'm not getting smaller."

Her gaze narrows. "So, I get that it's not the most fun way to spend the week before your wedding, but—"

"Haley's pregnant!" Serena blurts.

Ava blinks. "Well, shit. I mean, congratulations. You and Jax must be thrilled." I don't answer, and her mouth curves. "I will work my magic to make this waist lie flat."

She leaves the room, and Serena smooths invisible lines in my skirts with a half smile.

Her gaze meets mine. "I get that you didn't want to tell him over the phone from Philly, but you're back now, and the doctor said the risk of miscarrying has gone way down."

Nerves that have nothing to do with the pregnancy dance in my stomach, and I rub a thumb over the delicate lace there.

Inside, there's something—someone—Jax and I created together.

With all the stress of the wedding and the house earlier this spring, I missed taking a couple of pills. It was unlike me, but I figured it wasn't a big deal, so I didn't say anything to Jax before leaving for Philly.

But from the second I took the pregnancy test last month, my heart racing as I stared in shock at the blue line, it feels as if I've been living a secret life.

"You have talked about having kids," Serena prods.

"Yes, but we weren't planning on having them *yet*."

The first time I learned I was pregnant three years ago, Jax and I were split up. I was heartbroken and unprepared to raise a child on my own. At first when I miscarried, it seemed like one more scene of the same nightmare unfolding. But looking back, I can't help wondering if there wasn't some relief in the tragedy.

Serena squeezes my arm, bringing me back. "You've got this. Finding the right guy is the easy part. The rest of your lives? That's the real test."

"You're right." Her words bolster my resolve but can't quite strip away the worry. I always tested well in school, but this feels like a different kind of evaluation.

I take a deep breath, willing myself to focus on the excitement instead of the terror.

"I'll tell Jax tonight."

3

___

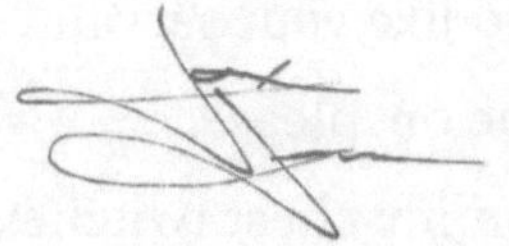

When I was touring as the frontman for the biggest rock band in the world, I spent twelve years telling people what to do.

Where to be. What I wanted. What I needed.

Now, my phone rings—Cardi fuckin' B no less—and I grab for it.

"When'd you change my ringtone?"

"Before we went to France," comes my spawn's breathless voice. "Aunt Grace and I went for lunch, but there was traffic. We're running late for the dress appointment."

"Serena'll have your ass."

"Serena loves me. We'll work it out."

I shake my head.

"I'm calling because I don't know if I forgot my hair straightener at the hotel. Can you check?"

"Do I sound like your servant?"

"Dad. Come on, please."

A muscle in my chest twitches. That's what happens when you become a dad—nature cleaves off a piece of your heart and hands it to a tiny creature who grows into a teenager with moods and demands and lip gloss.

I've made my peace with it.

But right now, I don't feel anything like free.

I'm already underslept, and not for good reasons, like because I was hammering out a track with some aspiring musicians for Big Leap or because Haley and I've been fucking each other senseless.

In fact, there's been *zero* action leading up to this wedding because my wife-to-be has been dealing with a bunch of paperwork in another city.

I'd had no idea my self-control was this low until I was forced to endure three weeks without Haley at my side, and in my bed.

This afternoon, she met my gaze over lunch with the caterers and my groomsmen and Nina.

Five minutes later, I had my tongue down her throat, fantasizing about my cock inside her and her moans vibrating against my hand so they didn't echo off the cars in my garage.

When Serena knocked on that door, I was ready to rip someone's throat out.

Because there's no combination of pleasures in the world that trumps the feel of Haley's soft skin, her sweet curves. The split second of hesitation the second I touch her, reminding me there's no one in the world she'd let do to her what I do.

When we were apart for two years, she took half my heart and carried it around in a backpack with her damned notebook computer. The past couple months she's spent looking after the selling of Cross's house and his last assets were an unwelcome reminder of that time.

This week is about closing the door on any lingering doubt that Haley's here and she's mine—now and forever. It's about knowing our future will be brighter than our troubled past.

We've been through hell. I'm determined to give her the heaven she deserves.

Satisfaction takes hold in my gut as I wind through the house to the foyer, where a dozen suitcases from friends and family still sit, waiting to be deployed to their rooms. It's like the boarding lounge of an airport.

I spot the suitcase in question—a lime-green one.

"Front pocket," Annie says over the phone as if she can see me.

"You could flatten your hair with an iron." I wedge the phone between my ear and shoulder as I yank on the zipper.

"Not funny."

The thing's stuck. How it's possible I can play "Mr. Sandman" on guitar in my sleep but can't get a suitcase open is beyond me.

"You guys working on your super-secret man project today? Tyler's pretty," she goes on at my silence, "but I offered him a Rice Krispies square for breakfast, and he folded like dough."

"He was up before noon?"

"We were talking last night. I might have fallen asleep in the pool house."

I picture my kid out cold on the couch, a blanket tucked up around her chin as she succumbed to the jetlag. Tyler on the other side of the room, snoring under the blankets.

A talented musician with his own family shit to shoulder, Tyler gets this life we have. Haley and I agreed he needed to be part of the wedding, so we paid for his travel from Philly, despite his arguments, and put him up in the pool house. Annie was ecstatic when she found out.

The zipper finally gives, and I reach inside. "There's nothing in..."

My fingers close on a packet that has my heart stopping.

"Dad? Did you find it?"

I step back, blink twice. It's still there in my hand. A shiny strip of evil.

"Dad?"

I clear my throat. "It's not here."

"...buy a new one, I guess. See you at dinner."

She clicks off, and after staring for another moment, I make my way out to the back patio and into one of the golf carts we rented for the week to get everyone around our massive property.

The tiny vehicle bumps over a hill, around a grove of trees. Another. It's June in Dallas, and the trees are blooming, birds are singing, and I'm officially beyond any of it.

When I cruise over the last hill, my gaze lands on a group of figures. Mace. Brick. Kyle. The guys from my band. The ones I've known for twelve years, the ones I'd trust with my life.

"There you are," Mace says, straightening and leaning the nail gun against the wood frame as I park next to the half-raised structure we've been working on for more than a week.

I take two steps in my work boots and snatch up a level in a grip that nearly breaks it. Kyle glances over from where he's sanding, and Brick folds his arms without dropping his hammer.

"Why are we building this again?" Brick asks.

"It's my gift to Haley." I take the nail gun and head for one of the columns.

"Jax. You need the verticals for that."

Every part of me stiffens, and I turn to lay

eyes on the kid Haley and I said we'd been thrilled to have at the wedding.

The one who's staying in the nice, private pool house because he prefers the more modest surroundings to the main house.

While my daughter has *condoms in her suitcase*.

The innocent picture of her sleeping on the couch a room away from him rips in half, morphing into something that leaves me snarling as I stare at the kid in front of me.

Tyler Adams looks as relaxed in the work boots I lent him as he does in scuffed sneakers. The faded denim and Pink Floyd T-shirt are his usual uniform. His hair is too long to stay back when he shoves at it, falling over his strong face.

In short, he packs a lot of swagger for seventeen.

"I'll do that," Tyler says, oblivious to my black thoughts.

My hand flexes on the nail gun as he reaches out.

He takes it from me, turning back to the gazebo. "I can nail in my sleep."

I don't know what a heart attack feels like, but I'm guessing it starts with the blood pounding in my chest, the pulsing painful enough I think something in there's going to rupture.

"You came down here to watch?" Mace quips.

I jerk my head to the side, and he follows me toward the steps.

Mace will talk me down. He's always had a soft spot for Annie, but despite his challenges since touring, he's level-headed and has settled into a routine.

"I found condoms in Annie's suitcase," I mutter.

Mace drops his cordless drill on the floor. "The fuck. You think Squirt and Tyler...?"

We both turn to take in the kid.

It can't be happening. I forbid it.

If it is...

"Murder's tough to cover up," Mace says.

Fire lights my stomach. "Brick'd lie for us in a heartbeat. Kyle's the wild card."

I watch Tyler work. He's too competent. No kid should be that musically talented *and* good at building things. It's not normal.

"We can't kill him, Jax."

There's the voice of reason, and I force myself to take a breath. "You're right. We're musicians. A hit would be cleaner."

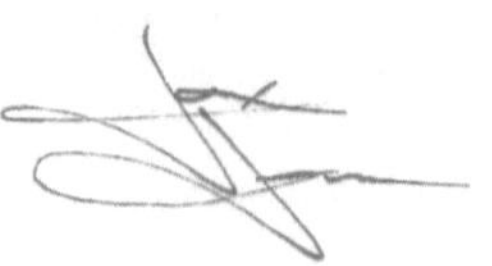

When we finish our work for the afternoon without bloodshed and head back up to the house, I still haven't decided what to do about my discovery.

I take a shower, scrubbing my skin until it's red.

Six hours ago, all I could think of was getting my fiancée alone. Now, I'm being tortured by problems other than my libido.

By the time I get back downstairs, most of the bags have disappeared from the foyer, and a group is standing around the island in the kitchen. It's like feeding time on the savannah. I look from Brick's, Mace's, and Kyle's intent faces to where Nina's unwrapping the food the caterers dropped off for dinner.

"There lobster, Neen?" Mace asks, sounding hopeful.

"Where do you think we are, a Michelin-star restaurant?" my former tour manager tosses. But as my friend's face falls, she relents. "Yes, there's lobster."

Brick steps up to help her. "Oh, babe. Chicken cordon bleu? You're a goddess."

"You say it like I made it," she grumbles but lets him press a kiss to her cheek before she ducks out of his arms with a smile.

Nothing tests friendships like having everyone you love in a house together. It's an old-as-time reality show concept for a reason. With everyone living out of suitcases and twenty-four-seven food—catering was a must—it's like being on tour again.

A tall guy with sharp eyes and light-brown hair, wearing a V-neck sweater and jeans, appears from the living room.

"Wes," I say to Serena's boyfriend, whom I vaguely remember was flying in from New York this morning. "Welcome to chaos."

He looks around the custom kitchen

with vaulted ceiling as if he can see through the walls to the other five thousand square feet of house and the acres of grounds beyond that. "I've taught thirty teenagers biology. I've seen chaos. This isn't it."

The guy seems straitlaced, but he has a confidence I like. As if he knows this isn't his domain but he's not intimidated.

"You heard from the girls?" I ask.

"Rena said they'd be back soon"—he checks his watch—"but not to hold dinner. I don't know Haley well, but if my girlfriend's looking at clothes? It might take a while."

Tonight, when Haley gets back from that dress fitting, I'm going to make her come so many times she forgets both our names.

Tomorrow, we'll finalize the vows with the minister at the church before getting some downtime with our friends for the bachelor and bachelorette parties Mace and Serena have planned.

Next, we'll run through the ceremony and rehearsal dinner at the church and estate where we'll be married on the weekend.

And before we know it, she'll be walking

down that aisle to me in the dress she's been hiding from me like it's her damned virginity.

Then flowers, cake, pictures, and faster than you can say, "I sure as fuck do," we'll be on a private plane to Bali.

Annie bounds inside from the patio, Tyler on her heels.

"Where were you?" I demand, looking her over from her toes to her dripping hair.

"Swimming." She lifts a brow, smirking at me. "We have a pool. Haven't you noticed?"

"The hell are those?" Mace pokes at one of the dishes with a fork.

"Fried pickles," Annie volunteers, leaping toward the island and grabbing a plate.

I'm not going to do my kid or my fiancée any good if I starve, so I grab a beef sandwich, then shepherd people toward the dining room with their piles of seafood, cold cuts, cheeses, crackers, pasta, and salad.

We've all found seats at the table, which can easily seat twelve but still feels full tonight, when Wes says, "So, I don't get how a celebrity wedding works."

"A celebrity wedding's nothing like a normal wedding," Nina starts. "One, the invites and seating arrangements are a beast. Every wrong pairing is a PR disaster waiting to happen. Some celebs just got divorced, and I'm not going to be held accountable for the fallout if they have to sit together. Plus, people are always offended they don't get an invite, even if you only met them at one Billboard awards, like, eight years ago.

"Which leads to two—people always show up who shouldn't be there. Who aren't invited.

"Three, it's impossible to control perception. No matter how discreet you think you are, someone takes photos they shouldn't, there are cameras places you've said they can't be, and people want you to look like a total moron."

"That sounds exactly like a normal wedding," Wes points out, and the room laughs.

But the hairs on my neck rise at Nina's description. Even though part of me knows it's true, none of those issues fits with the enjoyable experience I've promised Haley.

"Fuck the circus," I decide. "Let's have it on the patio by the pool."

Nina's gaze narrows as she holds up a fork.

"You don't mean that. The estate has been booked for months. The church too. Plus, there's no way you could fit that many guests on the patio, and everyone invited was instrumental to your career. It doesn't cost you anything to involve them in your wedding." A beat. "Well, between the church and the estate for the reception, plus the dresses and tuxes and favors and flowers and invitations, it costs you multiple six figures, but other than the money..."

She's right, and Haley and I decided together on the church, the venue, the guest list.

Still, I'm ready for things to be simpler.

That's another reason I was looking forward to Haley getting Cross's house sold and moving to Dallas. To move forward, to focus on our family, to leave our pasts and the industry behind.

The sound of the front door has me shifting out of my chair. My feet carry me toward the foyer in time to see Serena and Haley coming in.

"Sorry we're late. Some unplanned dress alterations," Serena says.

I look my fiancée up and down. "Impossible. She's perfect."

Serena wraps me in a hug. "You're a good guy."

"Tell me something I don't know," I grumble, but I like hearing it from someone Haley loves and respects, someone who shares my need to give Haley only the best life has to offer. "Food's in the kitchen. Wes's in the dining room. We haven't eaten him alive yet."

"Good. See that you don't." Serena disappears toward the dining room.

Haley looks up from taking off her shoes, her face flushed, her hair a dark curtain around her shoulders.

The sight of her makes every piece of drama, every angry thought in my mind, fall away.

She's the most beautiful woman I've ever seen. Always has been. Always will be.

"How was the fitting?" I ask.

"Good, until I started thinking about how much energy goes into making sure a garment I'll never wear again fits me to perfection."

Haley's always been down to earth, but I marvel at it again. I brush a kiss over her mouth that ends with my lips dragging up her jaw.

"It'll be worth it. You hungry?" I murmur.

"Not really, I…" She peers around me toward the kitchen. "Are those deep fried pickles?"

"I don't know how you smell those from here."

"Me either." In the kitchen, Haley grabs one and bites into it as if she's starving. "Oh, that's good."

I watch her eat, feeling a primal satisfaction that despite the hectic day, I can provide this small thing for her.

"How was your afternoon?" Haley munches.

I can just make out my kid seated next to Tyler in the dining room. I watch as Annie grabs food off his plate.

"Annie told me she crashed in the pool house last night. With Tyler."

Haley stops munching. "So?"

I frown. "So, she shouldn't be crashing with a boy. That platonic *Dawson's Creek* shit isn't real life."

"Dawson's what?"

"And even if it was, they ended up fucking eventually anyway."

Haley shakes her head. "I get that you're concerned. But I've never seen anything to suggest they're more than friends. We moved her to Dallas—"

"Back to Dallas."

"And separated her from her friend she's spent the last two summers with. It's a big change. Maybe they just need time."

"This is her home," I insist. "It's not like she's never been here before."

Haley looks past me. "That doesn't mean it's easy."

I debate telling her about the condoms but decide I don't want to stress her more. "I don't regret Annie, but sometimes? I think of how much simpler it was before."

Her lips freeze, parted. "But you want more kids."

If I'd thought today's events had killed my desire for her, all it took were those words —*more kids*—to have me craving her again.

It's twisted—I'll own that. I don't care. I want to get her pregnant. I want to see her pregnant. I want to know we've not only sworn ourselves to each other in front of our families, but God and the universe, by creating new life.

But after we've had time together first. Uninterrupted.

"I have a long list of things to do. Like relax. Enjoy this house. My new wife." I tug her between my legs, dropping a kiss on one of her temples, then the other, as if I can make the worry lines disappear.

But her expression doesn't warm like I'd hoped.

"I think I'm going to take a nap."

I search her face for signs of strain. "Tell me you're not getting sick."

"Just tired. I was up late working last night."

"I'll get away after dinner," I say at last. "We can *rest up* together." My tone makes it clear the last thing on my mind is resting, but her half smile has my brows rising. "You're going to dent my ego."

That earns me an eye roll that makes me grin. "Your ego has a decade of screaming, stripping women with 'Marry me, Jax' signs to bolster it."

"Mmm. But you're the only one who'd actually go through with it."

This time I get a full smile, and the tension in my gut eases.

"Did I hear Wes's voice on my way in? I should say hello."

"Hales. Go take a nap." I drop kisses around her face, ending with her lips. "And think of Bali."

"Bali," she repeats softly.

When I return to the kitchen after walking Haley to the foot of the stairs, someone's waiting for me.

Nina taps her phone against her hip as she leans over the island, lost in thought. She straightens the moment I enter. "We need to talk."

"What's going on?" Mace asks from the doorway.

"My office." They follow me down the hall, and I shut the door.

"You know what I said earlier about scorned people coming out of the woodwork for weddings?" she starts. "Something arrived in the mail from your ex."

Mace snorts, but I'm the one to answer. "I don't have an ex, Neen."

"The name Fiona doesn't ring a bell?"

Mace's eyes round on mine, and we say at the same time, "Fucking hell."

Every muscle in me goes taut.

"Show me," I command.

Nina produces a card with a New York return address. I break the seal and yank the card out of the envelope.

Congratulations on your wedding. - Fiona

"That's it? No other note?" I ask.

"Nothing."

"Ignore it," Mace insists. "It's a card."

"I haven't seen the woman in fifteen years. Not since—"

"Since she signed away the rights to her kid?" he says under his breath.

I haven't heard shit from Annie's biological mother in over a decade, which is exactly the way it was meant to be.

"Jax," Nina weighs in, "you and Haley have gotten thousands of cards. This is probably just one more."

She could be right, but I've lived my life assuming everything is a threat.

It's served me well.

Kept my family safe.

I reach for my phone.

"What are you doing?" she asks, alarmed.

"Taking care of it."

5

HALEY

FOUR DAYS UNTIL THE WEDDING

I haven't been to a lot of weddings, but I've always thought the vows were both restrictive and unromantic.

Good times and bad. Sickness and health.

A laundry list of "should do" items.

But now that Jax and I are sitting across the desk from the minister at the church Jax attended as a child, it occurs to me they're not restrictive at all.

They're vague.

Nothing in the vows tells you *how* to love another person. What to say to them when you can't quite meet their eyes, when the questions spinning in your head can't be spoken aloud because you're afraid of the answers.

I'd planned to tell Jax about the baby last night, but after what he said about Annie, I couldn't form the words. I stayed up reading in bed for an hour, but he didn't come up.

Then this morning, I stared at his handsome face while he slept. I was tempted to shift over him, drop kisses along his neck, traveling down his bare chest and further.

But I thought of the secret I'm keeping and felt guilty.

"What do you think, Haley?"

The minister's voice snaps me back to the church, and I silently berate myself for not paying closer attention.

"Ah. That sounds fine."

"'Love, cherish, and obey' sounds fine?" Jax raises a brow. "Lying to God on our wedding day seems like bad luck."

I shift forward, lifting the pages from the minister's hands and scanning them. "You're right. Is there something more contemporary?

Especially given this says nothing about Jax obeying *me*."

The minister shifts in his seat. "It is permissible to omit the word 'obey,' if you prefer."

"I think that would be best."

My fiancé coughs next to me, but the minister only nods. "Then that's all for today. We'll do the ceremony rehearsal with the wedding party tomorrow."

The minister shifts out of his chair, shaking Jax's hand and mine. Jax and I go to leave, Jax holding the door that leads to the main area of the church.

"What's on the agenda for this debaucherous bachelorette party tonight?" he asks.

Given the other weight on my mind, I hadn't given it a thought all day. "Serena said it's a surprise."

"Mace said the same. Been trying to beat it out of him for weeks. The guy's like a locked trunk."

I take in the beautiful church, the pews carved from some rich wood. I run a hand down the back of one as we pass it. "I have a hard time picturing you attending church."

"We did for a while. Not my dad. My mom and Grace."

"Before your mom's struggles with drugs?"

His amber eyes glint as his hair falls across his face. "And after. I think she wanted to make amends. Wanted to know that someone would forgive her."

I can relate to the desire to have someone look down on you and give permission. To approve on some level, if only to bring peace and certainty to the decisions it feels impossible to be certain about.

His face is surprisingly open as he peers at the rafters of the church, the stained window filtering light that spills crimson and gold and emerald into the chapel.

"I remember not wanting to come. Then once I was on the road, I missed it. Church felt like something normal people went to. People who didn't have to scrape themselves out of bed to be on the road at nine after a late stadium gig the night before."

I take in my future husband. His shirt's a button-down, covering up the tattoos on his arms. He's wearing jeans because no one's going to tell him not to, but despite the casual clothes, his body's tight underneath. From his tense expression, it occurs to me I'm not the only one in my head today.

His phone rings, splitting the beautiful silence, and he glances down. "I gotta get this." He strokes a thumb over my jaw, and I find a smile before he walks away.

I drop onto a pew, and by the time my butt hits the hard wood, my own phone rings.

"Haley," Nina says. "There's been some bad news. Jerry refused to get on the plane. I know he's never been a big fan of flying, but when we toured, he always used to suck it up when we had no other option. I was so sure we'd make it work this time, too." My body feels heavy even before she finishes. "Which means—"

"He won't make it," I say softly. I press a hand over my chest.

"We can find someone else to walk you down the aisle. It's not going to be a problem."

She tackles it like any challenge on tour, but when we hang up, my brain is numb. I lean back in the pew, the back digging into my shoulder blades. The man who's been like a father to me the past few years won't be coming.

This wouldn't have happened if we'd stayed in Philly.

I push down the thought. I agreed to the move. It was a decision Jax and I came to together.

He's been wanting to live here for years. His sister's here, as well as the house he bought after finishing his final tour, the one we've already been living in eight months of the year. It was a natural next step.

Still, Philly is where I grew up with my own mom. Where I went to elementary school, high school, college. It's where my father lived, where he built his business.

None of that was a real reason to stay. I'm not willing to trade Jax's future—our future—for my past.

I swipe at my eyes, which I hadn't realized were burning, and shift out of my seat, checking my email as I head down the empty row on autopilot.

Together with my business partner, I've built and sold four apps since college. Even though Jax has enough money to last us both a hundred lifetimes, work has been my challenge, my comfort, and my independence.

Six months ago, we got major publicity when one of our apps won a huge tech competition. Since then, there've been a number of new opportunities, but nothing next level.

That's why I pull up when I reach the aisle.

There's a new message from a client we've always wanted but never spoken to. One that would be a game changer.

I hit a number on my phone as a lone woman heads for the front of the chapel to light a candle. I turn my back toward the altar while the phone rings.

"Carter," I murmur when my business partner answers.

"Where are you, the library?"

"Church. I sent you an email. A major software company wants to work with us." I fill him in on the details. "They need proposals this week. I need you to put one in."

"No can do."

My jaw drops. "Come on."

"I do have a social life. In addition to traveling for your wedding. As much as I adore you, I can't drop everything at your request."

The arrogant edge works into his voice, the part that makes me regret ever sleeping with this guy—even when I had a mountain of evidence that I'd never see Jax again.

I curse. "Please? I did the last proposal while you were on vacation."

"Yeah, but you got to pick it. I get to pick the next one. Besides, I'm flying to Dallas tomorrow to see a few friends before the wedding."

"Carter, we can't pass up this opportunity." Desperation grasps at my insides. "Just think about it and get back to me."

As I hang up, Jax asks, "What was that about?"

I spin so fast I nearly trip over my own feet on the scarlet carpet as I take in my fiancé approaching. "A new client reached out."

Jax stops inches away, his gaze working over my face. "You spent the last month in Philly working. That must've earned you enough time off for your wedding."

Jax and I don't fight, but it's because I don't fight, not because he won't. Now though, I can't quite keep the edge out of my tone.

"Is that a suggestion? We did take out the 'obey' part."

"Everything all right?" the minister asks, and we both turn.

"Perfect, Father." Jax smiles tightly.

I turn and start down the aisle toward the doors. Jax falls into step with me.

I fill him in on the news about Jerry, and Jax curses. "I'm sorry, Hales. I know you wanted him to walk you down the aisle."

"It's fine. I'd rather he be at home where he's comfortable." I pause at the doors of the church and reach for his arm. "Hey, you want to take a drive before we go back to the house?"

"I have a meeting with the lawyer." He checks his watch before meeting my gaze. "But I can move it back."

I consider the offer as I stare up into his handsome, caring face. The man who's had my back, been my partner. The one I open up to like no one else.

I want nothing more than some time alone with Jax to let everything go...

But I can handle this.

I shake my head. "Don't worry about it. We'll talk tonight after Mace and Serena bring us home."

Jax bends down to claim my lips in a soft kiss that leaves tingles in its wake. Then he lifts a brow, a smirk on his handsome face. "*If* they bring us home."

6

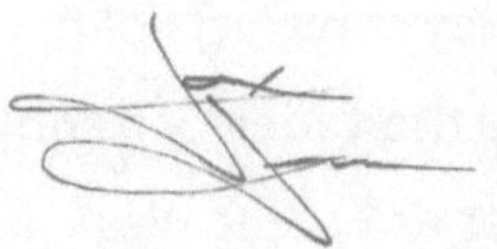

"**T**ell me that's not what I think it is."

I stare out the window of the limo as Mace, Brick, Kyle, Wes, and I pull up outside a dark building. The black sign has white neon lettering that says "Insiders."

Kyle grins. "It's exactly what you think it is."

"We're not going to a strip club."

"It's not just a strip club. It's the highest-end joint in Dallas."

Mace shifts forward, gesturing with a half-empty bottle of bourbon. "Come on, Jax. We came here once, remember? You turned twenty-one, and we had time off from tour."

"We dropped more money than I'd ever seen in one night," Kyle adds.

"We rented out the VIP room," Brick presses.

"And the booze is waiting inside," Mace reasons.

The fond way three sets of eyes have glazed over says this is their idea of a thoughtful gift.

I turn it over as I meet Wes's gaze.

I had one drink in the car, but after the day I've had, I'm looking to unwind.

When we got to the church this morning, I was feeling like shit about the shadows under Haley's eyes, the worry in her voice, the fact that by the time I got up to bed last night, she was fast asleep.

After dealing with Nina's revelation, I wanted nothing more than to lose myself in my fiancée's sweetness, to drown my frustrations in her moans and use every part of me to make her fall apart. But I'd have been a selfish prick to wake her for sex.

Still, when she got off the phone in the middle of the church where we're going to be married, it reminded me the reason she's been so tired is that she's insisting on working the week of our wedding. I know logically she's doing her job, but she's also the boss.

I was the boss on tour, but that was different. The dates were set in stone, sometimes years in advance.

Companies count on Haley to deliver them intelligent apps, but she gets to pick when she works and doesn't. If she wants to take time off, she can do it.

I've been trying to make everything perfect, and it's almost as if it's just another week for her.

The discontent lingered when I dropped her off and went to meet with my lawyer, who told me I was being suspicious about the card from Annie's biological mother.

He also assured me he'd look into it.

Because he knows the details of how it went down fifteen years ago and the NDA that was put in place to protect everyone involved. Just like he knows I can't afford to let it get out in the open.

"I finally have everything I want," I reminded him before leaving. "But it all goes up in smoke if I can't keep it."

"Jax." Mace's voice jerks me back to the car. "What do you wanna do here?"

Yeah, I need to unwind. But without naked chicks who don't have my ring on their finger.

I rub a hand over my jaw, which I forgot to shave this morning. "Tell you what—we'll grab the booze, then go somewhere else. Tell the driver to keep the car running."

I get out, sparing a glance for the lot filled with high-end cars, and the guys follow me to the back door.

"The place looks different," I note.

A woman in a black suit appears from inside, holding the door for us with a broad smile. "Gentlemen. We're so glad you've arrived."

We make our way inside, down a dark hall that opens to a plush room that's decorated with black walls and leather couches, simple crystal lights on the walls. Almost classy enough you don't notice the low stage in the center, the black velvet curtains separating it from whatever's beyond.

"We're not staying. You've got booze for us."

She gestures to the bottles behind a private

bar. There's a bucket with half a dozen bottles of Dom, plus every top-shelf bourbon I've ever tasted and a couple I haven't lined up along the ledge.

I nod my approval. "We'll take 'em to go."

"Oh. I'm so sorry, Mr. Jamieson. Our liquor license won't permit that. They need to be consumed on the premises."

The place is full of mirrors, but I see it with new eyes. It's basically a private bar. And it's all ours for the night. "We'll stay. But tell the girls they're not performing."

Her brows draw together. "The girls?"

"Ladies. Whatever."

"Ah, Mr. Jamieson—"

She doesn't have time to finish because hip-hop music blasts from some invisible speaker system, and the five of us turn at once toward the stage. The curtains have parted, and a line of men, greased up and half-naked, make their way onto the stage, gyrating to the beat.

"Shit, Brick. These are dudes," Kyle moans.

When I turn back to our hostess, she's been joined by a male bartender, shirtless with suspenders.

Yup. It's four days until my wedding, and all I want is to lock my bedroom door and fuck my absentee fiancée until she forgets everything that's not me.

Instead, I'm at a club surrounded by retired musicians and male strippers.

"We don't need the stage entertainment." One of the strippers, dressed as a firefighter, comes down off the stage and takes up a post between Mace and me. "Just drinks."

"Yeah, so let's cover that up," Mace says to the guy.

"I don't work out seven days a week to cover this up," comes his instant reply, winking at my friend.

I appreciate the irony that, after my day, this is what it takes to amuse me. I address the three men, who are costumed as a firefighter, a cop, and a cowboy. "Dance or don't dance. I don't care." My friends' heads all swivel immediately. "You'll be well compensated at the end of the night."

"We can't even try to convince you?" the firefighter asks.

"No," Mace and Brick echo.

"Hell no," Wes adds.

The firefighter meets Kyle's gaze and holds it. "What about you?"

Kyle hitches a thumb at the bar. "Dude, I haven't even started drinking yet."

I make my way to a couch, and my friends follow.

The bartender comes and pours us drinks. I can't help wondering if my abs look that cut from the side. I'm thirty-three; he's probably twenty-five, but still...

"To crazy adventures," Kyle kicks off the toast.

"To old friends and new ones." Brick nods to Wes.

"To futures as bright as our pasts," Mace adds.

After a sip of Bulleit, I say, "You guys did good on the drinks."

"Yeah?" Kyle looks hopeful.

"Do you think the girls are somewhere like this?" Wes muses.

I freeze, my drink halfway to my lips.

I motion the firefighter over from where he's hanging out at the bar with his, er, colleagues.

"Check the other room for a bachelorette party."

He grins. "There're a dozen bachelorettes, guaranteed. But don't picture your fiancée in there. Even if she is, I'm not gonna tell you she's thinking of you right now. But every other second"—his gaze roams my body—"she sure as hell is."

Wes coughs into his drink.

"Sit down," I offer graciously.

The firefighter drops down beside Kyle, the cowboy next to me, and the cop between Mace and Wes.

"So, we need a drinking game. How about 'I've Never'?" Kyle says, offering the firefighter a drink, which the guy takes.

"That's for college kids," Brick replies.

The cop lifts his hand. "I'm in college."

We start with easy ones.

I've never missed a show on account of puking my guts out. That one's for Mace.

I've never had a threesome backstage between sets. Brick drinks, saying, "You assholes better not tell Nina."

"Who do you think set it up?" Mace tosses back.

I've never left tour to chase a college girl across the country.

I drink twice on that one because I'd do it again.

And as far as getting us drunk, it works.

"I've never fucked someone in the wedding party," Mace declares with a sloppy grin.

I drink.

Brick drinks.

Kyle too.

As Wes drinks and sets down his glass, I wonder what he sees. We're a bunch of dudes who made our living in front of a crowd, making people feel something. He's a strait-laced guy, the book-smart type who can solve any problem, who not only understands the world but seeks to make it better.

"Okay, I know about Brick and Nina," Wes states, pointing at Kyle. "Who else is a couple that I don't know about?"

Ah, fuck.

Kyle realizes at about the same time. "Uh. Nothing, man."

Wes might wear dress shoes and button-downs, but if he knew Kyle and Serena had hooked up, he'd probably beat the shit out of my drummer.

Mace intervenes, turning to Wes. "You do computer shit like Haley, right? But some kind of matchmaking?"

My friend draws Wes into an explanation of his dating app, which the strippers seem fascinated by, peppering him with questions.

Listening to Wes, I see why he gets along with my fiancée. Haley's mind's always trying to find problems, to solve them.

"That how you and Serena met?" Mace asks.

"Yeah."

"She's cool. We used to see a lot of her in Philly."

"Some more than others. She and Kyle used to hang out a *lot*." Brick says this without thinking, and Wes's face darkens. "Kyle even went to yoga with her a few times."

Wes's gaze lands on my drummer. "Yoga," he echoes.

"Yeah," Kyle fills in quickly.

"Only yoga."

Kyle shifts in his seat. "It wasn't serious, man."

Mace tries to keep the peace. "One time."

Kyle winces. "Actually, a few times—"

"Kyle, shut up," Mace warns.

Wes tosses back the rest of his drink. "I'm gonna go. Excuse me."

He heads for the door without looking back.

Brick smacks Kyle's head. "Way to go."

"You're the one who brought it up."

Mace looks at me. "Think we should go after him?"

I turn it over. "Nah. Let him work it out."

Serena's going to murder my band, but I'm not worried. Kyle was a blip on the radar. Wes is the real thing.

Love like that lasts. It's what we spend our lives looking for, whether we know it or not.

"Women," Brick says, nodding for the bartender to grab another drink.

I can agree with that.

I've never asked my band for advice about women, but something has me saying, "Haley's been acting weird."

"Weird how?" This is from the firefighter, who's stroking Kyle's knee and doesn't seem at all perturbed to be asked to weigh in.

I narrow my gaze on him. "A word of this gets out, I will have your ass."

"That a promise? Kidding. We're discreet."

I shift forward, staring past them at the empty stage. "Haley's always got her own shit going on, and I love that about her. But this is different. The last month, she's been in Philly. I figured she'd come back and everything'd be normal, but..." I think of her troubled expression last night. The tension in her shoulders today. "Something's up."

"You think she's having second thoughts?" Brick asks.

In truth, I'd figured she was caught up in a work problem she couldn't solve. The possibility that it was something bigger, that she could be reconsidering all of it...

My gut tells me that's not it. I know she loves me.

But even the slimmest shred of possibility makes me want to rip this building from its foundation, strippers and all, and hurl it across the parking lot.

"This rich guy in my frat," the baby cop says, "proposed to his girlfriend. She dumped him the week before the wedding. Turned out all she wanted was the ring."

"Haley has the ring," I say under my breath. "And she's not like that."

The flawless five-carat diamond was half the size of what I'd wanted to buy her, but I knew she'd never wear anything bigger for fear it'd catch on something or mess with her typing rhythm or something equally practical.

Though her eyes had gone huge when I presented it to her, I knew in my soul that every ounce of that emotion was for me—not the rock.

"She has everything," I insist even as I rack my brain for something I've missed. "The house. The wedding..."

"You." Firefighter arches a brow, and I frown at him.

"Obviously."

He lifts his hands. "Just saying." His gaze runs over me, a grin tugging as his mouth. "If I were her, I'd say that's the best part."

Cowboy weighs in for the first time in a while. "In my experience, it's not about the trophies. Women want to know you'll go through hell for them. Marriages can be voided. They want it in blood."

We all stare at him for a long moment.

Then I glance at my arms and the ink along my skin.

In blood.

I straighten, snapping my fingers. "Get the limo."

7

HALEY

"Grip is important," the woman, who looks like Scarlett Johansson in full-on Black Widow mode with her leather pants and vest, explains. "Hold it firmly. Put your lower body into it. Then let the rotation do the work."

"That's what he said," Serena murmurs, and I swallow a laugh.

The woman releases the axe with a grunt, and it flips, end over end, until it lands with a satisfying *thunk* in the target ten feet away.

"I didn't know you could take axe throwing classes."

"It's not the most common bachelorette,

but after the move and everything else, I figured you might want to release some pressure. In a healthy way."

"It's perfect, and I love you."

It's true. I can't think of anything better than simple fun with my girlfriends tonight.

After Jax dropped me off this afternoon, I answered a few emails on a project I started this spring and have been trying to finalize before the wedding.

When I was in Philly, I decided I'd take another run at the Big Leap funding as a wedding present for Jax. I found some new sources and spent every spare moment writing up proposals and lobbying.

Jax outdoes me at most things. But staying just inside the rules while dazzling bureaucrats with how music education could expand with access and technology—that's something I can do for Jax. Something I'd love to do for him.

And I can't wait to find out if we're successful so I can tell him.

Since I was already in my email, I snuck another look at the proposal requirements for the client I learned about yesterday.

Then, because it didn't look that hard, I

started an outline and sent it to Carter while I was under the blow dryer at the hair appointment Serena insisted I needed to "freshen everything up."

Now, we finish our round of instruction—Serena's first axe makes it to the target, but it takes me and Nina two tries each—and take a load off with non-alcoholic drinks, including straws bent into little ring shapes at the top.

"I can't thank you enough for planning the wedding," I say to Nina when she takes a seat on the couch next to Serena and me.

"Are you kidding? Even if you weren't paying me—which you are and a lot—this event will be my calling card. Besides, I thrive on hard work and zero sleep, and I already have the overdeveloped biceps from managing tours." She flexes with her phone arm with a laugh, and her sheer competence is a relief.

"So, you and Brick. How long did that take to happen?" Serena asks Nina.

"Too long. But we were on tour. Working together. I couldn't do it then."

Serena laughs. "Wes and I hooked up even though we worked together."

"Everyone thinks musicians are crazy, but I hear the guys in suits are freaks."

Serena lifts a shoulder, her mouth curving into a smile. "What can I say? The man is high-strung. I like helping him unwind." She cocks her head. "What about Jax? Tell us, oh almost-married one. Is the sex getting predictable now that you've been together more than a year?"

A flush crawls up my face. "Um, no."

Both Nina and Serena burst into laughter at my expression. "That's all you have to say? Fine, use your hands. Thumbs up means it's better. Two thumbs up means it's way better."

I set my drink down on the table and glance around to make sure Annie's out of earshot of this conversation.

Then I stretch both hands as high as they'll reach, both thumbs pointing toward the ceiling.

Somehow, it's getting hotter. I'm living my own personal wicked fantasy—a man the entire world wants, and he can't get enough of me.

"Remember when the idea of a guy going down on you was hell?" Serena reminds me when her laughter dies down.

Nina chokes, and I bite my cheek. "I came around."

"Yeah, I bet you did."

Serena pokes her straw into her drink and lets out a little noise of irritation. "These ring straws are cute, but they don't hold up to repeated uses." She lifts it out, glaring at the frayed end.

"Maybe you're drinking too fast," I tease her.

"Not possible." Serena snaps her fingers. "Tyler! Can you check the car and see if we brought more of these?"

We'd decided Tyler was one of the girls since Brick and Kyle stated he was too young for whatever they were planning.

The guy in question looks up from where he's talking to Annie in the corner.

We watch him depart, and he returns a minute later with a bag. "Here you go." He tosses it at Serena, and she catches it with a grin.

"Thanks. You need a new one?"

Tyler lifts a brow. "Do I need to drink my Coke through paper bling? Nah, I'm good."

My lips twitch as I watch as him return to

Annie's side. She says something I can't hear, and Tyler reaches a hand into the ice bucket in front of them, dropping enough ice into her drink to make the contents splash.

She shoves at his shoulder, and he grins as he reaches for his own drink.

"Oh, high school." Serena sighs. "First crush, first everything."

I straighten in my seat, thinking about Jax's concerns from earlier. At the time, I brushed them off, but maybe I was too dismissive. "How old were you? For your first everything."

"Sixteen."

I glance at Nina.

"I lost my V-card at fifteen."

I sip on my own ring straw as I turn back to the kids.

Jax has been Annie's primary parent since the three of us started living under the same roof. While we discuss issues with one another, at the end of the day, I try to respect that she's his daughter.

But even though Annie doesn't often come to me with her problems, I've always tried to be there for her. And it's understandable that sex isn't something she'd seek out her dad to talk about.

I'd always figured something might bloom between Annie and Tyler, but I'd also assumed we'd know before there was. That they'd go out on a date or we'd spot them cuddling or kissing.

Instead, they seem like good friends. The kind of friends you want for your kids.

We would know, I insist to myself.

But before I can process that further, Nina bounces up. "Ready for round two?"

I watch her get another axe from the Scarlett woman.

The sound of an axe sinking into a target chased by a loud groan has us looking over. Nina's holding her shoulder and bent double.

"Shit!" I gasp, leaping up to run over to her. "You okay?"

"I think so, but it hurts."

The Scarlett woman's there in an instant, inspecting Nina.

"You might have sprained it," she says, and Nina's eyes widen. "But I'm no doctor, and it's probably best you get checked out at the hospital."

The five of us pile into the limo.

"This was a bad idea," Serena says, dropping her bag and Nina's on the seat beside her. "I didn't mean to break the wedding planner."

Serena reaches into the bar on the inside of the door and unscrews a tiny bottled shot of bourbon. "For the pain."

"I don't drink much," Nina protests. "Herbal tea mostly. My alcohol tolerance is low."

But as Nina shifts in her seat, she lets out a low moan and grabs her shoulder.

Serena starts to recap the bottle, but Nina interrupts. "Wait."

With a brief hesitation, Nina takes it from her and tosses the whole thing back in a gulp.

"Is it helping?" Serena asks.

"It's doing something."

Serena pours a shot for herself and something sugary for Annie, Tyler, and me.

"Why aren't you drinking, Haley?" Annie asks.

"Ah, I have to get up early tomorrow."

"We all have to be at the church at ten."

"Right. But I need to, um, wax," I supply,

cursing in my mind the moment the word slips out.

"But you say waxing's for swimmers and masochists," she counters.

"And special occasions." I focus with renewed intensity on Nina's shoulder. "When you threw it, did you hear something pop?"

"I'm not sure." She touches the shoulder gingerly with a hand. "But I think that drink might be helping."

Nina reaches for another bottle and drains that one, too.

When the car stops at the emergency room, we start out of the limo, but Nina grabs for the third bottle on the door.

A male nurse looks up from his clipboard as we approach the registration window inside the emergency room.

"What is that?" he asks, nodding toward the bottle in Nina's fingertips.

"Pain management."

"You can't bring that in here."

I expect her to protest, having watched her negotiate with the biggest venue owners in North America and go head-to-head with producers and CFOs over tour budgets.

Instead she nods solemnly. "I understand."

Nina looks around the triage room filled with a dozen other patients and their loved ones.

Then unscrews the lid and drains the bottle.

8

HALEY

When we get home, it's after three and no one's awake on the main level despite the lights being on in the hall and living room.

We get Nina set up in a spare bedroom to avoid her getting jostled by Brick, who's snoring and taking up the entire bed in theirs.

By the time I head to my room, exhaustion is setting in, along with the reality that our wedding planner is drunk and half-maimed down the hall.

As I turn the handle carefully, I prepare my eyes to adjust to the blackness. But as I push the door in, there's a light on in the corner.

Our room's large and sprawling. A master

suite at its most extreme. An en suite goes off one side. A walk-in closet that's the size of my bedroom when I was in college goes off another door. There's a sitting area at one end with a full-sized couch, coffee table, and chairs, plus the four-poster king bed in the center.

My fiancé's sitting, asleep, in his favorite wingback chair by the huge window.

"Hey," I say softly, closing the door behind me.

Jax twitches in his seat, straightening so his gaze meets mine. "What time is it?"

"Almost four. When'd you get home?"

"Couple hours ago. You have fun?"

"It was more extreme than I imagined. Nina dislocated her shoulder." Both Jax's eyebrows rise in tandem. "The doctors set it, put it in a sling, and told her to be careful over the next few weeks. We tried to shush her with painkillers and talk of subcontractors."

"Did you guys have fun?" I ask, fully taking in my fiancé for the first time.

He's wearing a tight, black T-shirt and blue jeans, the same uniform that hooked me years ago. The angle of that jaw is perfect, masculine and square, hinting at the stubbornness that drives me crazy even as I can't help but respect it. His muscled shoulders and chest and forearms make my throat dry.

Sharing space with Jax always affects me. I've never ceased wondering at his ability to arouse me, agitate me, and calm me at different times.

Tonight, his simple presence soothes my nerves.

I bridge the distance between us, my sock feet sinking into the plush carpet.

Jax lifts his chin, somehow managing to look as if he's staring down at me even though he's sitting. "It was... revealing. We ended up at a strip club."

Every tired muscle in me tightens as I stop in front of his chair.

I can deal with the fact that women throw themselves at my future husband in part because he never throws himself back.

Now, the vision of half-naked women dancing anywhere near my fiancé has me furious.

"Tell me you're joking." There's no mistaking the edge in my tone.

Jax leans forward, deliberate, his amber

eyes glowing on mine. When our mouths are inches apart, he stops.

"It was a male strip club."

I blink, confused. "I don't understand."

"Me either. If they guys ask, tell them I loved it." He grins, and before I can pull back, his thumb brushes my lower lip as he murmurs, "But I like seeing you jealous."

My anger slips away a bit at a time, replaced by a pulsing need in my veins as he looks at me.

My fiancé—husband, soon—is fucking hot. He's also fierce and determined and devoted.

"What's that look?" he asks, curiosity entering his expression, the hint of a smile curving his lips.

"You."

Jax's eyes flash as he drops his gaze down my body and back up. I'm glad I wore tight faux-leather leggings for the axe throwing thing and that I'd decided the evening wouldn't be physical enough to warrant a sports bra and opted for a push-up under my white tank.

"Back at you, Hales." His voice has lowered an octave.

That voice that had me from the start. Even before I knew him.

The voice that seduced millions of people. And he's looking at me. He's all mine.

I climb into his lap, straddling his hard thighs. Jax's chin tilts up, his eyes darkening to glowing embers on mine. His hands slide up my thighs to my ass, tugging me possessively against his groin, where there's growing evidence we're desperate for the same sweet relief.

"We should probably be figuring out how to manage without our wedding planner," I murmur.

"Someone's getting married?" His joke is a rasp as he looks between my eyes and my mouth.

Lust overtakes me, a wave that's been building in strength these past days. Weeks.

I need him, the man I love, but I also need the release only he can give me.

He's on the same page, but when I lower my mouth to his, his hands grip my hair, holding me a breath away. "Hales, I can't go slow tonight."

His beautiful voice is raw silk against my lips.

"Good."

I crush my mouth to his.

Jax isn't content to let me lead. His grip on me tightens, and he grinds me against him as if it's his right to use me however he wants.

It's dirty and arrogant.

I love it.

He's going to have to peel these pants off me because beneath them, I'm soaked.

But if I'm desperate, Jax is ruthless. He devours my mouth, tasting every inch of me before dragging his lips along my jaw, scraping his teeth down my neck until I whimper and press closer. My fingers stroke down his chest. His grunt ends on a hiss as I reach his abs and jerk his shirt up high enough that I can press my palm to his cut stomach and feel it twitch under my touch.

It's not enough. I need assurance from his body that I'm not ready to ask for with my words. That no matter what happens with me, with us, it's going to be okay. We're going to be okay.

I sigh against his mouth as I trail my hands

along his hot skin, my fingertips playing with the trail of hair right above the button of his jeans.

Before I can protest, he lifts me without effort, my breath catching as he carries me to the wall and sets me on the floor.

"Every inch of you is mine." His rasp is hot on my neck as he yanks on the waist of my pants, stripping them off with impressive efficiency.

He drags a hand up my thigh, under the panel of my panties that're already soaked, and I hiccup a breath at the feel of it.

The sound of tearing fabric has me gasping as I look down to see he's ripped my underwear clean off.

Nope. The sex has not gotten boring.

I reach for his shirt, intent on beginning my own assault, but he pushes my fingers away, reaching under my top, flicking the clasp of my bra, and cupping my breasts, rolling my nipples under his skilled fingers.

Oh my God.

Madness has me reaching for his jeans only to find he's already got them open. His cock is there, huge and hard and straining against my hand.

I wrap a hand around his cock, loving the way his nostrils flare.

Whatever little control he was clutching snaps.

Jax devours me with a "Fucking hell, Hales," against my mouth that's more vibration than words.

He positions himself between my thighs and, without warning, slides home in a single stroke.

I moan from the feel of him.

"Fuck, you're so tight after a month without me," Jax groans as he fills me, stretches me in that way that makes me gulp oxygen as I struggle to adjust. It's uncomfortable but so good, and I moan at the contrast, the duality of it. "If you're not quiet, they're gonna hear you."

"They know we have sex," I pant, tightening my grip on his neck as if I can keep him from withdrawing.

"But now they're gonna know you're so—" He pulls nearly all the way out, then thrusts hard enough my entire body shudders around him. "Fucking." Again, my nails dig into his shoulders. "*Ruined for me.*"

This time I cry out, from the feeling and the knowledge that every part of him, every inch, every atom, is in this moment.

I used to wonder what true physical intimacy felt like.

Now I know it doesn't matter whether we're slow or fast, gentle or rough.

It's overwhelming and intoxicating. It's knowing there's something in this world bigger than you, beyond your control...

But that same wondrous thing would miss you, would be irrevocably changed, if you left.

Jax builds a rhythm I couldn't resist if I wanted to.

When we both come, it's explosive. The entire world craters, and the only thing that's real is the pleasure throbbing through my core, along my arms and legs. Even my lips are tingling.

I swear it takes minutes for me to feel my fingers and toes again.

Jax is still panting against my throat when a loud buzzing has our heads jerking toward the nightstand, where my phone screen is lit up.

I can just make out the name. *Carter.*

Jax stiffens as he sees it too.

My muscles tighten in warning, the intense physical release forgotten in a heartbeat as he reaches for the phone.

Jax glances at the message before holding it out to me.

Just looked at the proposal. You must be determined to do this deal. You write that at the salon between manicures?

I can't help cursing the bad timing. I left my phone on because I wanted to be available if Jax or one of the guys texted and forgot to turn it off when I arrived home. "Jax—"

When I look up, Jax's face is dark with accusation. "I know you've been distracted lately. I get it now."

"You do?" My hand drifts to my bare stomach, and I feel exposed in a way that goes far deeper than my nakedness.

"I figured you were stressed with all the wedding details, but your head's not even here.

You're thinking about work and Philly, every-thing except for us."

His voice still low but guarded now, the opposite of the intimacy and adoration from a few minutes ago. The words land heavily on my heart, each one a stone that dents and bruises.

"That's not true," I insist.

"Isn't it?" Jax crosses the room to the closet, emerges a moment later with pajama pants, and yanks them on.

I watch him stalk across the floor to the bedroom door. "Where are you going?"

"I'm too worked up to sleep."

"We have the ceremony rehearsal tomorrow at ten."

Jax cuts me a long look, his jaw still ticking. "I'll be there."

9

THREE DAYS UNTIL THE WEDDING

I wake up in an unfamiliar bedroom with pale-gray walls, alone and with a kink in my neck.

It takes a moment for me to catch up to where the hell I am.

When I remember last night, I almost wish I hadn't.

I don't regret the sex. The way Haley and I tore at each other was hot as fuck, and as I pad toward a mirror, I can see the evidence in scratches on my shoulders, bruises under the ink. It was incredible, though it was also supposed to be the warm-up round. It's barely made a dent in the pent-up reservoir of need I have for her.

But we were interrupted when I noticed the message from Carter.

I know I overreacted, but that's how I am. That's also why my first stop when leave the spare room and start down the long hall is our room.

My fiancée's asleep in our massive bed. Despite the fact that she's alone, her body's curled on her side as if leaving room for me.

My chest contracts as I cross to her, take in her pale face. Her hair spilling across the pillow.

I drop a kiss at the corner of her mouth that has her moaning softly.

I'm not mad at her. We've had disagreements before but nothing I could hold on to in my heart.

Because, I've realized over the past few months, my heart belongs to Haley—she's the only one brave enough, bold enough to hold it.

After getting dressed quietly so I don't wake her, I head to the kitchen to grab a coffee and glance at Nina's hard-copy hotel room list for our guests.

When I've got the info I need, I hop into my Bentley and take off down the driveway.

At the hotel, I go right to the first-floor room and knock.

No answer.

Again, louder.

I start back down the hall, glancing into the gym, and I stop. I jerk open the door and stalk inside to where Haley's business partner is on the treadmill.

"Jax."

"Connor." I deliberately say his name wrong because it's what we do.

In theory, I see how he'd be attractive to the wide-eyed freshman class, with the hard part, glasses that are probably fashion over form, a too-white smile and hair so light he must spend more time on a beach instead of in his office.

Haley's way too smart to get caught up in that.

"When we invited you to the wedding, I didn't expect you to say yes," I go on, pleasant.

"Haley and I are close. I couldn't have said no."

"You could've."

He lifts a shoulder. "I could've. I wouldn't do that to her."

The fact that he thinks he has the power to do anything to her chafes. But I keep my irritation in check because I have more important matters to focus on.

"Haley's got a new client she wants to work with. You can take care of it."

"You think because the world bows at your feet, you can tell me what to do?" He gets smugger. "I know you're arrogant, but this is another level."

The prick looks like a rodent, but who knows—maybe he's open to reason. "We both want Haley to be happy. But at the moment, her life is more complicated than it needs to be."

"Haley's life? Or Haley? Maybe she's more complicated than you gave her credit for."

The glint in his eye has my hands fisting at my sides.

A few years ago, there would have been no chance I'd walk out of here without laying him flat on his back. Now, I take a deep breath as he continues.

"You can sweep her off her feet. You can take her to Dallas. Hell, you can even marry her. But you'll never control her."

"I didn't come down here to control her," I state, a deadly calm coming over me. "I came here to tell you that if you are business partners, you will act like you own a pair and deal with this and let her have this week."

"And here I thought you just needed a more intense workout than in the pool. I hear it's harder to stay in shape after thirty."

I hit the up button on his treadmill a few times, kicking his pace from nine miles an hour up to eleven.

"I can only imagine how hard it is to stay in shape locked in your ivory tower and listening to teenagers bitch all day."

Sweat drips from his brow. "It is. Haley spends her days in front of a computer. I don't know how she stays looking like that."

I hit the up button some more.

Twelve.

"I help her out. With that and *anything else* she needs."

My finger hovers over the button as Carter's eyes widen.

I press it again.

Thirteen.

By now Carter's wheezing, his legs churning under him in a satisfyingly stilted way.

He hits the down button until the treadmill stops.

He grabs for his water bottle, but I snag it first.

"The harder you squeeze, the more she's going to slip away," he says, trying not to pant. I unscrew the lid slowly, peering inside at the water. "Haley's the most independent woman I've met. That's never going to change. Not even for you."

I look at him, my face deliberately blank.

What was it Haley said when we got screwed out of that Big Leap funding?

"Don't burn tomorrow for today. They may not have sided with you on this one, but it doesn't mean they won't another time. Listen to them; show them you appreciate what they have to say."

I can do that. But her style is more easy-going than mine, so I decide to ad lib.

"Thanks for the advice, Connor."

The smugness melts from his face as if he's equally shocked by my words and friendly tone.

Then I dump the contents of the water bottle over his head, taking a moment to watch the water pour off his hair onto the treadmill belt before I turn to leave.

"**W**hy the hell isn't he answering his phone?" Nina demands, then winces as she holds her good arm over her stomach as if it's shifting inside.

She takes in the narrow-eyed minister a few feet away. "Sorry, Father. I'm not used to being hungover."

I glance toward the doors of the church as if my fiancé will walk in any second. "He said he'd be here."

I bite my lip and try Jax's cell again. It rings four times before his voicemail kicks in. "Maybe we can do the walk-through without him and fill him in once he arrives?"

No one looks excited, but we do it anyway.

"Brick and Annie walk first," Nina says, her voice fainter than usual. "Then Serena and Kyle."

"Why not me and you?" Kyle asks Nina as Serena offers her arm, his usually affable face constricted. I swear he cuts a nervous glance toward the pew Wes is sitting in a few rows back.

But Serena's boyfriend is working on his phone.

"Because I want to be the last person down to make sure all the details are looked after," Nina says.

Everyone does their thing, Nina a wan presence lurking over us. She told me in the car on the way over that she tried to take her prescription pain meds this morning but couldn't keep anything down.

"Haley, you sure you don't want someone to walk you?" Nina asks.

I nod, thinking again of Jerry and how much I could use his sense of humor and perspective right about now.

"Okay. Start from there."

I take my place at the doors and count to

four before starting down the aisle. My gaze roves the empty pews, and my fingers hook in my belt loops as I think of all the people who will fill those seats in a few days.

"You need something to hold on to." Serena fishes in her bag, producing one of the tiny liquor bottles from the car last night.

Nina makes a retching sound, covering her mouth with her hand.

"Here, Haley. Pretend it's flowers."

That's how I end up walking down the aisle of a church toward the gaping hole my fiancé, who refused to sleep in our bed last night, should be occupying.

Oh, and I'm pregnant and clutching a mini bottle of hard liquor.

When I get to the end of the aisle, the doors bang open behind us. Relief has me sagging when I see Jax stalking toward us in a dark-blue button-down over jeans.

"Well. Look who decided to show," Nina says on a wheezing breath.

"The hell happened to her?" Jax demands.

"Long story. I'm glad you're here," I tell him.

His cloud. "Yeah. Me too."

As we rehearse the ceremony, my mind keeps escaping to how we left things last night.

I understand how Jax could read me working three days before the wedding as being distracted, but he doesn't understand why.

Because you won't tell him.

Still, I sent Carter an email this morning to say that if he didn't have time to work on the proposal, I understood. We'd let this opportunity pass and wait on the next one.

"Haley?" The minister prompts. "It's your words."

"Sorry?"

"To love and cherish."

Jax's gaze works over me. The accusation from last night is gone, but there's assessment in its place, as if he's searching for an answer that's under my skin.

"All right," the minister says when we finish, as if supremely relieved we've made it this far. "Why don't we take a break before running it one last time?"

"I'll be back," Jax says before turning and starting toward the side of the church.

"I've got him," Mace says under his breath before following.

Serena falls into a discussion with Kyle and Brick over the optimal walking speed and how to accommodate Nina's sling while Nina makes quiet inquiries with the minister after a garbage can.

Kyle inspects the altar, running a finger over the shiny surface. "Haley, does this look like rosewood to you?"

"Mmmm? I'm not sure." A sudden wave of tiredness washes over me, and I sink into a pew.

Annie sits next to me, nodding at my heels. "Wanna trade shoes?"

"You're sweet. Thanks. I could go for some water though. I think I left a bottle in the car."

We walk back down the aisle, and she follows me outside. I hit the locks for my car and reach into the back.

"You don't have to hide it," she notes. Her amber eyes are like Jax's but twice as perceptive. "I can tell you're pregnant."

I freeze halfway inside my vehicle, then pull back out with the bottle in my hand. "When did you know?"

"I've been wondering for a while. My dad doesn't know."

I take a long sip from the bottle. "No."

This morning I woke up feeling nauseous for the first time. It was a stark reminder of what's coming and the secret that still hangs between me and Jax.

The clock is ticking, but I won't drop this news when one of us is already frustrated with seating arrangements or catering or—worse—with the other.

"I also wasn't sure how to tell you."

"Because you thought I'd freak out?"

"Maybe." I take a sparkling water from the car and offer it to her. "I'd understand if you did. Freak out."

Annie pops the drink open and leans against the car next to me. "When I was little, I always wanted a brother or sister. There were times I wished I could share everything with someone."

My chest tightens with nerves. "And now?"

"The house has ten bedrooms. Besides, that'll get my dad off my case, right?" Her lips curve.

Relief hits me in a wave. I hadn't realized

how much I was worried about what Annie might think, but now it feels as though some small weight has been lifted.

Annie produces Ray-Bans from somewhere in her dress and tucks them onto her head. "What's it like? Being pregnant, I mean."

"Strange. Your body's not quite your own."

"What if men had to deal with being pregnant?"

The ridiculousness of Jax contending with physical symptoms has me chuckling. "There would be a lot fewer babies," I say drily. "Your father in particular would probably never reproduce."

"I think about that sometimes," Annie blurts. "My mom. The woman who gave birth to me. He's never told me about her."

I shift on my feet, my heels leaving holes in the gravel of the parking lot. "Me either."

"Does it bother you?"

"No," I say honestly. "I know that he was young and on the road and that she wasn't a big part of his life romantically. But in some ways, she'll always be part of him because she gave him you."

She tucks a piece of hair behind her ear, and I wonder what's going on in her head.

"Would you tell someone?" I ask her. "Your dad, or me, if you were having sex?"

She quirks a brow. "I'm not looking for sex tips from my dad and stepmom." I feel a flush crawl up my face. "Just because I know what you guys do together doesn't mean I want to know, you know...what you *do* together."

I hold up a hand, and it takes me a second to come up with an answer. "That's not what I mean." I must look super uncomfortable, because Annie laughs, and I can't resist smiling too. "But it's an important time. With a lot of change and a lot of feelings and a lot of big decisions."

"You wouldn't try to stop me?"

There's probably some right answer to this question, but I don't know what it is. All I know is that Jax and I both want her to feel supported and make the best choices she can. And we'll have her back no matter what.

I take a breath. "When my mom talked to me about sex, she never bullshitted me. I appreciated that. She said, 'If you're old enough to do it, you're old enough to decide.' I believe that."

"The first time you did... it wasn't my dad."

"No. Although it was different with your dad. Is different."

She lifts a hand. "Okay, leaving the region of girl talk and approaching the city limits of TMI."

I swallow a laugh.

"How did you know he was the one?"

I turn the question over in my head. "Every time I looked at him, I wanted him. Not physically," I rush as she turns green, "but I wanted inside his head. His soul."

As I say it, I realize it's true. We've been through so much together—the early days on his tour, how he opened up to me the way he wouldn't with anyone else. How he took the time to get to know me, a nameless intern. How even when there was no honest way we should have been together, he came after me.

And even when I left him, even when I pushed him, he never let go of me. Not in his heart. For every time we've struggled, we've come back stronger.

"He never does things the easy way, but he

fights for what he loves. And everything he does…" My mouth twitches at the corners as I remember things. "He's poetry."

Annie smiles a little. "You are to him, too. I never saw him look at anyone the way he looks at you. You're the answer to every question he has."

Surprise has me shifting, assessing her with new eyes.

Annie seems so young, but in some ways, she's nearly grown. In a matter of months, she'll be driving without supervision, taking AP classes, considering colleges.

"I guess we should head back in," she says before I can come up with a response.

I follow her up the front steps and into the foyer to search out my almost-husband, feeling a little lighter than I have in days.

JAX

"They'll be in this room, flitting around like butterflies," I tell Tyler, who's leaning against a column in the aisle off to the side, out of view of the chapel. "Everything a seventeen-year-old kid could dream of."

He looks at me, his brown eyes intelligent and serious. "You think I should introduce myself to one of the producers who'll be here for the wedding."

"No, I'll do the introducing."

Mace comes up beside us, and I nod to him to help.

"Err, yeah," he supplies. "You've been screwing around with Wicked and Big Leap for what, three years total? This could be your break. Land a contract. Go on tour. Every kid's fantasy."

There's been too much out of my control this week, and I'm remedying that right now. Carter was the first fix.

The second is the boy standing in front of me, looking between me and Mace with a mix of wariness and amusement.

I don't know what he's doing or not doing with my daughter, but there's an easy way to make sure it never happens: fill his head with dreams of stardom plus the means of getting there, and he'll forget all about my kid.

Tyler finally replies, "Who said a record deal's what I want?"

It's my turn to stare. "It's what every musician wants."

"It wasn't what you wanted," he tosses back, reminding me I was forced into it in order to keep my family fed and sheltered.

"No, but everyone I've ever worked with has been kind enough to point out that I'm fucked up like that."

Mace looks as perplexed as me.

For the first time, I think about how much I know of this kid.

I've spent time in the studio with him for more than a year. He not only helped me get Haley back, for which I'll be forever grateful, but he's also helped with the programming at Big Leap. Hell, if I was starting as a frontman today, I'd be lucky to have Tyler at my side.

He's talented. I wouldn't bullshit him about that. Even though we're in a church, my religion is music. It's my truth and my soul and everything real.

At seventeen, he has more possibility in his little finger than I ever had.

"You don't want to be famous? For everyone

to know who you are?" Mace adds. "You're insane. The attention. The validation. The money doesn't suck either."

Tyler looks past me in that way teenagers do, as if you're more air than flesh and they're considering things beyond your grasp. "I appreciate the offer, but I'd rather not have so much money I wonder if my friends are my friends. Where everyone wants a cut of you, no matter where they take it from. Where everything I care about is at risk of being taken from me."

Some people think all troubled childhoods leave the same scars. I know better.

The marks left by our parents, our families, our circumstances, are as unique as a fingerprint.

I don't know the details of his situation, but life experience tells me his jeans aren't shredded by a designer. The scuffed Converse sneakers were on someone else's feet before his. And despite it all, every time you put a guitar in his hands, he lights up like the sun.

My gaze works over him, thinking of the million questions I have.

I settle on one.

"What's wrong with your hair? Last time I saw it, it was blue. Hell, every time I've seen it, it's been blue."

Tyler rubs a hand over his neck. "Thought this might be more respectful. Since it's a wedding and all."

"Well," I say at last, "if you change your mind about meeting producers, you let me know."

"Sure." He nods as if we're peers. "But I won't."

As Tyler walks away, Mace says, "What the hell was that?"

I stare after the kid. "An interesting development."

Tyler talks like he doesn't give a shit about the world's temptations. The fact that he changed his look means he cares about fitting in with our family. He wants to do the right thing, even if he's not sure what that is.

This past week, I've been worrying about him and my daughter.

But this changes things.

"Any word from Fiona?"

Mace's voice drags me back.

"Got a call from the lawyer on my way over.

It's why I was late. She insisted it was a card and nothing more."

"You don't think she's out of the picture?" Mace echoes my doubt.

My hands tighten into fists. "Not when a track on her phone shows she's in Dallas."

I've barely gotten the words out when a loud voice drags our attention back to toward the pews.

"What the hell, Brick?" Serena's gesturing wildly with the iPad Brick was playing games on earlier.

"I didn't mean to tell him!"

She throws it at him, and he catches it inches from his face.

"If it's not a big deal, why are you freaking out?" Wes's usual calm voice is raised.

"I'm not freaking out. You're the one who sits on this all night, then ambushes me in the middle of a church!"

"Right. Because my girlfriend slept with a rock star in the wedding party and didn't tell me, and I'm in the wrong here."

My head swivels, trying to find Nina.

I spot her dress on the far side of the pews, where she's bent over what looks like an urn, emptying the contents of her stomach.

Haley and Annie are frozen right inside the doors.

I stalk toward the altar, trying to figure out how to get this all under control, when Kyle's voice grabs my attention.

"This church in Dallas supposedly helps its fellow man, but does it?" Kyle strokes the altar, tilting his camera phone down. "This altar is made of rosewood, an endangered tree species with an illegal black market trade worth millions of dollars a year."

"What is going on here?!" the wide-eyed minister interrupts before I can take charge, his voice shaking as he surveys the scene.

"No shouting. This is a place of worship. And that urn you defiled is an antique!" he screeches at Nina, wresting it from her hands as she guiltily meets his gaze.

"And you!" He stalks toward Kyle. "No social media exposés." He knocks the phone from my drummer's hands.

"We are finished for today. Everybody out!"

"Father—" I say.

"I need you out from under my roof."

Wes moves up the aisle, and I'm grateful for a voice of reason as he stops in front of the minister.

"I thought it was God's roof," Wes says.

Mace and I exchange a look before the minister's face turns purple as he points a shaking hand toward the doors. "*Out!*"

11

"Well, that was interesting," Annie says as she drops into a lounge chair on the patio.

Serena sits next to her, Wes hovering between them. Tyler takes a seat on the low stone wall a few feet away, and Brick, Kyle, and Mace find seats too. We're all facing one another except Nina, who stands next to the pool, staring at the surface.

The drive back was near silent, as if we were all stunned we had been kicked out of a church.

"I need to make some calls," Nina says, reaching for her phone with her bad hand and cursing as she realizes what she's done.

"No." Jax's low voice rumbles as he emerges from the patio doors. "What we need is to get on the same damn page. This week hasn't been easy, but we dealt with bigger problems on tour all the time."

"It's true." Serena shifts out of her chair, nodding to Nina. "You've run tours your entire life, and you want to plan weddings. The shoulder thing sucks, but you're living your dream." She turns to Mace, Brick, and Kyle. "You guys are the best band on the planet. You've always been there for Jax. This shouldn't be any different." Finally, she takes in Wes, who's eyeing her with a combination of longing and mistrust. "I know this week has come with some surprises, but we all have a history, Wes. That doesn't mean we'd repeat it."

"She's right," I say, and every head turns to me. "Every wedding comes with its share of craziness." I take in my almost-husband. "Ours was bound to have more than most.

"What we need is to take a break," I decide.

Jax's eyes harden on mine, and Serena sucks in a breath.

"Not you and me, Jax," I hurry to add. "All of us. Today."

"How?" Mace asks.

"Haley, there's so much still to do," Nina adds. "Decorations and final check and—"

I hold up a hand. "I understand. And I will pitch in to make sure everything comes together, even if that means setting up flower arrangements and laying out table numbers. And I know Jax will too."

Shock and horror cross Nina's face. "Absolutely not."

I wave her off. "The point is we're family. Everyone here has been through it together. We'll do this together, too."

Before anyone can respond, Jax reaches into his pocket for his phone, staring at the screen in annoyance. "What the...?"

"What?"

"C'mon." He hits a button, then starts toward the house. We all follow, trailing him through the main floor and spilling out onto the front porch to find a giant van pulling up the driveway.

Not a van. A *bus*.

A familiar bus with the words *Big Leap Studio* lettered on the side. My heart's thudding even before the driver's door opens and sunglasses and red hair appear. A woman steps out wearing a boho sundress and the biggest sunglasses I've ever seen.

"We're here!" Lita shrieks.

I'm down the steps before I can put together coherent thoughts, and my friend and Jax's former opening act wraps me in a huge hug. "I thought you were on tour this week!"

"We managed to find a couple days' wiggle room," she says, beaming as she pulls back.

Her words catch up to me. "Wait, you said we. Who's we?"

She rounds to the passenger side and opens the door. "Jerry."

I run to the old man and grab his frail form in a hug.

"The man really doesn't like planes," Lita says drily as my eyes fill with tears.

"It's flirting with death even before you eat the food," he gripes, and I hold him tighter.

"Hi, Jerry."

"Haley," he says when I pull back, and my chest swells so big it could burst.

I want to say I've missed him, that I'm beyond glad he's here, but he'd call that sentimental crap. So, I settle for memorizing the comforting feel of him, the lines of his face.

Jerry cuts a bleary look over my shoulder. "This the hotel? Where's my bellhop?"

Tyler steps forward and grabs one of his suitcases as Jerry rounds the bus, surveying the group standing on the porch.

"Why the hell's everyone so down? We didn't sell out the show?"

"There's no show tonight, Jerry," Lita says, but Jax holds up a hand.

"Course we did," he says. "We're Riot Act. You remember the last time we didn't, old man?"

"Fall of '06," Jerry pronounces.

"Nebraska," Mace, Brick, Kyle, and even Jax chorus with him.

"I've got it," Mace blurts. "Two words: Granada Theater."

I have no idea what that means, but everyone else seems to.

Brick and Kyle exchange a look. Even Nina drums the fingers of her good hand on her lips as her expression lightens.

"It's short notice," she says.

"It's us," Brick points out.

"It's good." Jax's vote is the deciding one.

I don't know what's been decided, but anticipation hums in the air.

"What's the Granada Theater, Uncle Ryan?" Annie asks Mace as he pulls out his phone. I'm as curious as she is.

Kyle waves a hand over the tableau of bewildered, frustrated people. "Exactly what we need."

"We're watching a concert?" I ask as we pile out of the Big Leap bus in front of a repertory theater with a marquee.

The past two hours, the guys and Nina have been on the phone and busy doing... something.

"Close." Jax has changed from the button-down shirt into a black T-shirt and jeans and white sneakers. He follows me down the bus steps, stopping on the sidewalk next to me.

"Nice kicks," I can't resist commenting.

He produces an Astros ball cap and jams it down on his head. His grin makes my heart beat faster. "Had to go through a few boxes to find 'em."

Annie points at the marquee. "Look! Jason Ryker's playing."

The guy's a mashup of country and rock, but I know him.

Mace is right—a night of hanging out together and enjoying a great band could be the perfect thing.

I start toward the front door, but Jax's hand finds my arm. "Wrong way, Hales."

We round the building to the back door and are immediately welcomed. The guys disappear backstage, probably to say hello. They know everyone in the industry.

Jerry and I head toward the front of the house with Annie, Nina, Serena, and Wes.

"Jerry!" I call over the noise as I realize he's stopped behind us. I go back to get him. "Come on. Let's go check the sound."

He grunts but complies, and we get settled in a booth by the stage.

When the band comes on, we cheer, but the guys still aren't with us. I glance past the band into the dark wings, and given the angle of our table, I see a familiar ballcap flash at the corner of the stage.

I lean over to Annie, who's sitting next to me.

"They can't watch the whole show from backstage!"

Annie cocks her head at me. "You don't think they're going to *watch* the show, do you?"

I'm still processing her words when Ryker's Texas drawl drags my attention back to the stage.

"Thank you, Dallas! Now, before we sign off, I have an outrageous surprise for you that I take full credit for."

As he talks, his band unplugs and a roadie runs out to make adjustments to the equipment.

No, they're not...

Kyle steps to the drum set, twirling a set of sticks in his fingers as the excited buzz from the room yields a few shrieks and "oh my God"s.

I exchange a look with Annie, and she grins.

Mace and Brick walk out next, slinging guitars over their necks.

"No fucking way," Serena blurts. "When was the last time they played together?"

"Not in ages." Excitement and disbelief have my chest swelling. "Jax hasn't even messed around with Big Leap since he got the bad news about funding."

The next person on stage isn't one I expected, but a hand grabs my arm—Annie's—as Tyler strides out, hooking a guitar around his neck. He doesn't even look at the crowd as he adjusts some settings before plugging in and straightening his mic, one of three and the nearest to our side of the stage. Then he shoves a hand through the dark chunk of hair falling across his lean face.

If there are any teenage girls in here tonight, Annie won't be the only one watching him.

"What do you think it's like?" she breathes, her eyes locked on the stage.

"What what's like?"

She turns big eyes on me, wide with anticipation. "Being up there."

I haven't had time to process my surprise at her response when the lights cut.

The crowd screams, and a thrill races

through me. Instantly, I'm twenty-one again. The world doesn't exist beyond this venue, this room. Beyond the molecules in the air, vibrating with potential and promise.

A spotlight cuts the darkness, illuminates the center of the stage, and screaming rips the quiet in two.

Because there's Jax, taking up the entire stage with his presence, his physicality. It's a wonder there's space for anyone else, for instruments, with his broad chest and shoulders, his cocky stance, his hard jaw and blazing amber eyes.

He doesn't count off, but I know the second before the band breaks into their track, before Jax's low voice that the world has paid hundreds of millions to hear fills the room.

"Bass is off. I need to fix it," Jerry complains over the music.

But when Jax wraps his hands around the mic, all I can think about is how it feels when he wraps his hands around me. I'm throbbing with need.

Lita's hollering, Annie's applauding, and even Wes looks impressed. Because it's impossible not to give in to these guys and the music they create.

I scan the room, the screaming fans, lucky women fumbling with cell phones to capture this moment that Jax Jamieson and Riot Act reunited after years apart.

I get it. I feel it too.

I remember every part of being on tour, of learning the trade, of falling for Jax.

Emotions roll through me. Fear, anticipation, longing, desire. They collide in my gut as past blends with present, memories and possibilities dancing in my mind.

My hand rubs my stomach lightly as "Redline" heads into the final chorus, then rests there as the final chord hangs in the air to thunderous applause.

"You think she knows?" Annie asks.

I lift a brow. "Her?"

"Come on. It has to be a girl."

Tingles work through me as Annie turns back to the stage with a smile.

I glance to my other side and see Serena looking between the stage and the bar, the direction Wes is disappearing toward.

Reluctant to miss a second of the show but

knowing I need to, I tap her arm before jerking my chin toward the hall.

She follows me to the bathroom.

"You guys okay?" I ask once I've shut us both inside.

Serena's face scrunches up. "He's being weird, Haley. I mean, he's always weird—he's Wes. But this is different. I hate that he's not talking to me. He has to know he has nothing to be threatened by. Wes is smart and sexy, and he's worth a thousand Kyles."

Empathy has me squeezing my friend's arms. "Maybe he's not threatened. Maybe he feels like this isn't his world. I still feel that way sometimes."

"It is his world. This week it is because it was mine. And we're together now. How can he not see that?"

"You could spell it out for him," I suggest with a half smile. "I'm not the most qualified to be handing out dating advice—"

"Actually, you bagged a rock star. You're the most qualified to be handing out dating advice."

I roll my eyes. "Anyway, when men try to

guess what you're thinking and feeling, it usually ends badly for everyone."

She blows out a breath. "I'll talk to him. What about you?" Serena squares her shoulders, staring me down. "You told Annie you're pregnant, but you still haven't told Jax?"

I brace my hands on the vanity. "It's strange. I remember this one morning a few years ago when I slept through my alarm on tour. I was in a panic, my entire body shaking, because I missed catching a car to the venue for the concert that night. It was all I could think about, all that mattered, because I knew Jerry would chew me out. The only thing I cared about was doing my job, getting my course credits, succeeding in school."

It seems so far away now.

"Later, I was in Jax's change room backstage with him and he gave me his hoodie." My skin tingles at the memory of pulling it on, of feeling the soft fabric against my skin, of smelling his masculine scent up close. "And I swear I felt it."

"What?"

"My life expanding."

I shiver thinking of it now.

That tour took me from being a starry-eyed kid to knowing I could take control of my life. That I get to make my choices and live with the consequences.

"Now, I feel like my life's exploded again, only I missed that moment. And it's crazy, but I swear if I could pinpoint the second it happened, if I could understand it—" frustration has my fingers turning white on the sink "—I'd know how to handle all of this.

"But in three days, I'm marrying Jax. In a few months, we'll have a baby together." I swallow. "I can be a coder, Serena. I can be a fan. I can even build a business or date a rock star. But now, I'm supposed to be a wife and a mother, and I don't know how to be those things. What if I don't have it in me?"

The dull roar outside the door hangs between us as Serena stares at me with compassion. "Don't worry about it until you have to. You're Haley Telfer," she reminds me. "You'll always be Haley Telfer, and no matter where you live or who you're married to? That won't change."

Her words ease the knot in my chest a few

degrees, the feeling that the ground under my feet is shifting yet again.

As we find our way back to the seats and the band starts another song, I decide that for tonight, I don't have to have all the answers.

"What are you doing?" Serena demands as my fingers dig into her shoulder to help me boost myself up onto the table.

"Enjoying the show," I tell her before straightening.

Jax's gaze meets mine, his eyes dancing with approval.

I cup my hands around my mouth, and with every other living thing in that room, I scream.

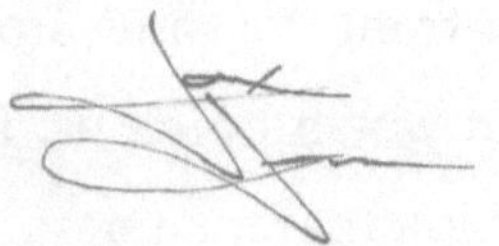

12

Nothing feels like being on stage. As I make my way to our crew, it's still thrumming in my veins—the power, the creation. It's been a long time since I've felt that way, and the adrenaline is addictive.

Nina hollers, "Boys, you've still got it."

I stop in front of Haley. Her face tips up to me, her lips full and eyes big.

Jerry's voice breaks into my thoughts. "You were all right, but the—"

"Bass was too loud," Mace and I echo.

Brick throws up his hands.

I grin, still looking at my fiancée. "Well?"

She steps closer, breathless. Her fingers

trace my arms. "Not bad considering you're retired."

With a groan, I claim her with a kiss that's one part love for her attitude and one part punishment for it.

I get a high from the show, from the music, from the crowd worshipping us. But since her, hers is the opinion that matters.

She's the one I want saying my name. The one that makes it all worthwhile.

"Break it up. That's what the honeymoon is for," Serena teases, but I take my time before stepping back.

Then the group of us sits and drinks and talks. We catch up, hearing about Lita's drive from Philly with Jerry, and the tension that's been hanging over the week eases a few degrees.

Eventually we pile into the bus to drive home.

Inside, Mace starts toward the studio in the back, but I grab his shirt. "Everyone stays up here. My bus, my rules."

Catcalls go up, and Haley flushes as she tucks a piece of hair behind her ear.

But she shrugs with a smile. "Sorry, boys. It is Jax's bus."

The fact that she agrees with me, even on such a small thing, sends a surge of satisfaction through me.

The crew drops onto the couches up front as I grab Haley's hand and tug her toward the back—the studio where my bedroom used to be when this was my tour bus.

We shut the glass door that separates the studio, then I pull the curtain over it. It's silent back here, and the only sensory stimulus seeping in is the cushioned gliding of the bus moving over the streets.

Haley looks around the studio. "You built all this from scratch?"

"Me and the guys. Jerry weighed in on the tech." I follow her gaze to the soundboard, the amps and mics and soundproof walls we installed with our bare hands. "Been awhile since I was in here."

"Getting denied that funding for Big Leap hit you hard."

My chest twinges, but I shrug as I run a hand over a panel of wall filled with Sharpie signatures

—one from every kid who spent time here. There are close to fifty, but I want hundreds. "Like you said, it's nothing personal. A bunch of bureaucrats pushing papers. They don't know music. They don't know what we do, why it matters."

But her gaze works over mine. "Don't give up on it. Not on those kids and not on you. Just because things don't happen the way we expect doesn't mean they won't happen."

Her words soothe the ache inside me that hasn't gone away since the news. The part of me that wonders if I fucked it up somehow, if I let those kids down.

I pull her toward the couch on one side of the studio. She stretches out next to me, and her body lying over mine is comforting and arousing at once.

"Tonight was something else," she says. "Do you miss it? Being on stage."

"Being on stage is good." Half my mind is already on the feel of her against me, wondering if I can get her naked before the bus pulls up to our house. "It's everything else that's bullshit."

Haley lifts herself over me, one arm on

either side of my head and a curtain of hair shielding us from the rest of the studio.

"It doesn't have to be that way."

I reach up to stroke a thumb over her cheek, thoughts of what I want to do to her temporarily paused as I huff out a breath. "Hales, I've been on the top of this industry, and the more venues we packed, the more I was at its mercy."

"You're Jax Jamieson. You don't have to be at anyone's mercy."

I tug her against me, kissing her deeply.

I love how she sees me. I'm not only a face, a name—I'm a man. She knows when to remind me I'm mortal and when to tell me I'm invincible.

Haley's the first to pull back, but I keep her close enough that our breath mingles.

"You should've seen Annie tonight. She wanted to be up there."

Few things catch me by surprise, but this does.

I turn over the presence of Annie's birth mother and multiply that by a thousand when Annie's the one in the spotlight. I curse as protectiveness bristles through me.

"I don't want that for her. It's a dangerous dream."

Haley's lips curve over mine. "I'm starting to think life is a dangerous dream."

Before I can turn that over fully, there's a knock on the back window.

"We're back at the house, so we're heading out. We'll leave the door unlocked," comes Mace's dry voice through the gap in the frame.

Haley calls back her thanks.

I stare up at the ceiling and the little glow-in-the-dark star stickers that were Kyle's contribution to the studio's decorations. After we renovated, he insisted on replacing them on the new ceiling—an ode to the past.

"I always dreamed of having a gazebo," Haley murmurs, fitting her curves against my hard body and tucking her head into my chest. "Sitting out in it at night. Did I tell you that?"

"No."

Yes.

"There's something about sitting outside with the stars that's so simple and beautiful and romantic. Nothing we can create is as awe-inspiring as what already exists, but that's not a reason to stop trying."

I could listen to her talk all night. It's one of my favorite things about her, the way she thinks. I know she doesn't let many people into her head, and I'm endlessly humbled and amazed she lets me in.

"That's why I started coding. The idea that we can construct music that moves us, deep down, so that we can call on that kind of wonder whenever we want…"

"Sounds like being a god."

"More like being an engineer. A god creates something from nothing. You were always a god to me, Jax. You always had that power, and you wield it with more grace than I've ever seen."

Christ. The emotion her words elicit has my ribs expanding until I swear they're going to crack. Her fingers trail over my heart, and I swallow the ache, capturing those fingers and holding them still.

If this woman ever leaves me, I don't know what I'll do. She's the only one who sees me. The only one I want to go through everything with.

I could live without money, without fame,

maybe even without music. But without her... I don't ever want to feel what that's like again.

"So, tomorrow's the rehearsal dinner," she whispers. "I'm sure everything will go smoothly."

"Have we learned nothing from these past few days?" I tease, and she bursts out laughing.

"Let's enjoy tonight."

"Uh-huh." I pull her mouth to mine and kiss her, hard.

But I need so much more than the feel of her sweet lips opening for me. I need to claim every inch of her, inside and out, to remind us both she's mine.

In my head, I know I get to have her like this for the rest of my life. That knowledge does nothing to reduce the urgency inside me, the conviction that if I don't claim her tonight, I've lost.

I kiss her with that inexplicable need, and she moans as my tongue strokes hers. I skim my hands down her sides, memorizing each slow curve of her breasts, her waist, her ass, as if I might never get to touch them again.

Haley kisses me back with the same sweet fervor, impatient hands grasping the bottom of my T-shirt and yanking up. I chuckle against her lips as she strips my shirt over my head.

She rears back to look at me, her hungry gaze lingering on my hard abs before dragging up my chest. I want to tell her to hurry up, but I also want her to take her time. I see her mind working, devouring each inch of me, see the desire and overwhelm on her face.

Music made me a king. She makes me a god.

Her gaze halts over my heart, her smile freezing.

"Jax? What is that?"

I shift up on my elbows, cocking my head at her. My pulse pounds in my throat. "A tattoo."

Dark, hazel eyes search mine as her throat bobs.

"'HJ,'" she whispers.

"Haley Jamieson."

I don't have to look down to picture the tat I got after the bachelor party, the letters entwined with one another, a script font.

But she's staring at it as if it's a snake.

"What's wrong?" There's an edge under my tone.

Her throat works. "I'm not changing my name, Jax."

The words echo in the dark.

The bubble we've been living in, the simplicity of these hours together, evaporates.

I flip her in a heartbeat. For the first time, I'm regretting the semi-darkness because I need to see more of her face. No, I need to see into her *soul* right now. "What are you talking about?"

"We didn't discuss it," she says quietly.

"We didn't have to. You're going to be my wife."

"I've already had two last names. I'm not in a rush to add a third." Her hands find my shoulders, but her touch has cooled from a second ago.

Frustration has my hands falling into fists on either side of her head. "You think nothing's going to change when we walk down that aisle?"

"Everything's already changed. In the last two years, you launched an album, we started a charity on wheels, I sold my father's home, moved into a new house in a new state."

"Something changes when we get married, Hales," I warn. "What changes is you're mine."

Mine to take care of. Mine to worship. Mine to keep.

She lifts her chin, eyes imploring me. "I'm already yours. This wedding doesn't prove anything. I love you, more than I thought I could love anyone. But I wasn't waiting around for you to save me. I..."

"What?" I force the word through my tight throat.

"I'm still me without you."

The words are daggers in my soul.

I shift off her and fall back against the couch. The stars overhead aren't comforting anymore—they're cold.

Even though our arms are touching, even though she's a breath away...

There are miles between us.

Because I feel as though the one woman I gave everything to, the one I want to give everything to, is about to hand it back.

13

———

I hate sport coats. They're the devil.

But Nina sent over clothes for the rehearsal dinner, and by the time I finished taking out my frustration on the outdoor project, I didn't have time to pick something else.

"Nice jacket," Mace comments, pulling up beside me.

I shoot him a withering look.

"Gotta say the place looks good," Mace says. His long hair's slicked back tonight, though he bucked the sport coat in favor of a crisp white shirt.

"It's not good," Nina retorts, breezing past in a blue dress. "The cake we were promised is delayed. How does a cake get delayed? It's baked, or it's not."

The rest of the girls are scheduled to arrive at the estate where we're hosting the reception in their own car. Mace, Brick, Kyle, Wes, Tyler, Jerry, and I rode over ourselves. I glance at my phone.

"I get why Neen's on edge, but what's got you so worked up?" Mace asks.

"I showed Haley the tat on the way home last night. She was... surprised."

Mace curses. "Not a good surprise, I take it."

I narrow my gaze. "Not a good surprise."

We didn't fight last night, but I went to sleep feeling heavy. Despite being back in my bed, Haley curled in my arms, the tattoo over my chest was a weight.

A reminder that everything I want is within my grasp and it's still slipping away.

Jerry appears at my elbow.

"Jax, I hear someone's getting married," he informs me.

"God knows," I say, only half joking.

With that, the women walk in the front doors. Haley looks beautiful in a knee-length black dress, her hair swept over one shoulder.

Before I can approach her, Nina calls us all to order. "Dinner will be served in thirty minutes. You have time for one drink before we go over the details of how the evening and speeches will run, so make it count."

I make a beeline for the bar and order a bourbon.

Annie drops into the seat next to me at the bar, taking a moment to adjust her dress. "Tyler said you offered to set him up with producers. Why?"

I lift a brow. "I'm a nice person."

"You're not that nice."

"You gonna tell her?" Mace shifts his elbows onto the bar on my other side.

"Tell me what?" Annie demands.

"He found your condoms, Squirt."

Silence hangs over the bar, the bartender freezing mid-pour before turning his back on us to give some semblance of privacy.

My daughter shifts out of her seat, straightening to her full height. "Dad? Explain."

I reach for the drink the bartender sets in front of me, then on second thought, set it down. "They were in your suitcase." I meet her fiery gaze. "The green one."

Annie shakes her head slowly. "I don't have a green suitcase. I haven't in two years. I gave it away to—"

"My green suitcase?" We all look over at the sound of Kyle's voice.

Fuck me.

Annie makes a choking sound. "You found condoms and thought they were mine, and instead of asking me about it, you what, decided to send Tyler away?"

Pretty much.

"Wow. We're friends. It is possible to have friends of the opposite sex, you know. Though I can see why Haley doesn't tell you anything."

That comment has me straightening. "Wait. What doesn't Haley tell me?"

But Annie's already stalking toward the bathroom.

I want to tear after her, but Lita's voice pulls me back. "Where's Jerry?"

I pull up halfway across the room, my gaze scanning the bar, the table where Haley's still talking with Serena, and the corner where Nina's gesturing wildly at Brick as if they're playing some awful game of charades. "Where *is* Jerry?"

Lita and I go outside and down the front steps of the restaurant, past the venue security hired to stand watch.

"You seen an old guy?"

"He went that way." One of the men gestures down the road.

"And you didn't think to stop him?" I holler. "Fucking great. Jerry!"

Leaving Lita with the guards, I go after him.

My shoes slip on grass that's damp from sprinklers, but I don't care. I stare into the darkness as I pace the grounds, starting with the parking lot and working my way farther out.

I don't look back to see if anyone's joining me.

Those security guys are going to be out of a job.

After a few minutes, the irritation's gone and panic has fully taken its place.

I'm scanning a treeline when I see a

familiar hunched outline.

"Jerry. Jerry!"

He looks up the second time I call his name, and when I run to meet him, he narrows his eyes.

"How'd you get all the way out here?" I demand, trying my best to inspect him for injuries in the dark.

"Needed some breathing room." His thin voice is decisive. "It's stuffy in there. I don't know why we booked that hall. It's a terrible place for a show."

I grunt, relief edging in as I realize he's fine—physically, anyway. "It is a terrible place for a show," I agree.

No matter his mental state, or how soaked my shoes are, I'm grateful to be standing with the man who's seen me through years on the road, helped me deal with a decade of triumphs and heartaches.

"It's also a terrible place for a wedding."

His voice sounds more lucid than it has since he arrived. "I never got married. You know that. But a wedding's like a good mix.

"The biggest array, the best board, the latest toys can't do what true intimacy can."

I turn that over, thinking of one of the first conversations Haley and I had on tour. "Leonard Cohen at the Orpheum."

"Leonard Cohen at the Orpheum," he agrees.

A breeze lifts the fine hairs on his head, and I glance down at his dress shirt.

I shrug out of my sport coat and help him into it, fastening the button over his too-lean frame so he doesn't get cold.

"You're giving me your jacket?" he asks in a tight voice, inspecting the sleeves.

"Don't tell Nina."

"Worse. I'll tell Haley. Make her jealous."

I laugh under my breath, shoving my hands in my pockets. "She'll understand."

"She understands most things. If I ever found a woman like that, I would've got married."

"I'm sure you would've." Despite his condition, Jerry understands more about life than I could hope to. It's why I can't resist continuing. "But no matter how close I hold her, I'm on top of the world one moment and helpless the next.

"I've been out of the industry more than a

year, and I keep waiting for the moment I feel like I'm in control of my life."

His wheezing laugh carries through the night until I'm concerned he's going to bust a lung.

"Jax, you were never in control. Control is an illusion men create to avoid the truth."

I lift a brow. "What truth is that?"

"That every single shit you give makes you that much more vulnerable."

His words settle into me. "God knows why any of us risk it."

"Because we aren't meant to be all knowing, all powerful. We're meant to *feel*. With love comes fear. With gain comes loss. Your only choice is this: are you in or out. For all of it."

I turn that over as I stare at him, his frail form. The eyes cast in shadow that I know better than my own. The ones that can be bright one moment and bleary the next.

"Are we going back?" he asks as if I'm the one who brought us out here.

I glance back toward the lights of the estate, soaking in the stillness around us.

"Another minute."

I stand in the dark with him.

I've finally gotten Jerry back up to the estate house and given the security guards shit again for not stopping him from wandering off when my phone buzzes in my pocket.

"Father, this isn't the best time." My hand tightens on the phone as I listen to him. "Are you kidding? We said we'd pay for the damages."

He speaks again, and my eyes squeeze shut.

"There's nothing I can do to convince you?"

I listen to his firm words before hanging up and making my way back toward the doors.

Haley's there to greet me, her expression troubled. "Jax, Jerry's back with Mace and Brick. Is he okay?"

"He's fine."

Her body sags in relief.

"I phoned the police after you left to see if they could come out and help search," she says. "They told me they don't usually do that sort of thing, but they had a car in the area and promised to stop by."

"Good thinking."

The relief on her face is replaced by nerves.

"Jax..." Her throat works, and the tension has my chest tightening in turn. "I need to tell you something. It's not the best time, but I can't keep it from you any longer."

She steps closer, drawing in a breath and holding it, her anguished eyes searching mine.

Immediately, my call with the minister is the last thing on my mind. It's nothing compared to the worry on her face right now.

A dozen possibilities flash through my mind, each worse than the last, ending with one that turns my stomach to stone: she's changed her mind about the wedding. About us.

Grief and denial twist inside me, and I regret every harsh word I've uttered in the past week. I'd take it all back in this moment. "Hales, listen to me—"

"I'm pregnant," she blurts.

The words spill out, settle between us. My brain turns them over once, twice but they might as well be another language.

None of the scenarios playing through my head a moment ago were anything like this. This is...

Impossible.

"You're pregnant," I echo at last.

Haley's throat bobs as she nods. "Twelve weeks. It happened before I left for Philly. I missed a couple of pills by accident. I've never done that before, and I didn't think it would matter."

I soak in her expression, but her words are drowned out by the hammering in my ears.

Haley's pregnant. It's what's been causing the shadows under her eyes. Why she's looked so stressed. Why she won't talk to me.

"Will you please say something?"

That phrase penetrates my thick skull, and I blink back at her.

But before I can answer, the doors open behind me and a too-familiar voice interrupts. "Haley!"

The hairs are already rising on my neck before I turn to find Carter in the doorway.

The security people here will never work again.

He crosses to my fiancée, and every muscle in me strings tight with the urge to hurl him across the room.

"You weren't answering your phone, so I had to come down here. You were right about this contract, and the bid is due tonight. We don't submit by midnight, we'll lose our shot."

"Chris..." Haley trails off.

I don't wait for her to finish. Every ounce of my rage and frustration crystalizes into the blond pinhead that is Christopher Carter.

I roll up my sleeves, then grab him by the collar of his shirt, pushing him toward the door.

"What are you doing?" Carter spits as I shove him out the doors.

"You're trespassing. I'm removing you."

The security guards straighten, snapping to attention.

"This isn't your property," Carter presses.

"No? I could buy it with a snap of my fingers," I say, the cool night air hitting my face and adding to the adrenaline coursing through me. Flashing lights appear on the horizon, but I barely acknowledge them. "But that would be a waste because by then, it'll be over."

"What will?"

"This."

And I hit him.

Hard.

14

HALEY

Everything goes crazy from the second Jax's fist connects with Carter's face. Our friends are shouting, bodies rushing toward or away from the scene.

The police cruiser I called for halts at the foot of the steps, doors slamming as two officers dash toward us.

I can't move. I'm frozen even though I'm screaming at myself to do something.

It's the security guards who pull Jax off Carter. The blood on my business partner's face finally jolts me into action.

"Are you okay?" I ask Carter as he sits on a stair, his eyes spacey.

"No! I'm fucking bleeding."

"We need a cloth," Serena barks from somewhere behind me. "And some ice."

"I think his nose is broken," says Nina.

Ice and a cloth appear, and I make a homemade compress and hold it to Carter's face.

"Why are you here?" I demand.

Carter lets out a pained sigh as he shifts back on an elbow. "You were right. This bid was big. We need to finish it."

I gesture around us. "This is my rehearsal dinner, Carter!"

His gaze moves over me as if for the first time. "And you look gorgeous."

The earnest comment is so out-of-place, I suddenly empathize with Jax's desire to hit him.

"Hold this." Instead of indulging, I pass him the ice pack as I search out Jax with my gaze. He still hasn't reacted to my confession.

Finding Jax's tattoo last night was confirmation that everything around me is changing, and the world isn't giving me a chance of keeping up.

But the expression on his face when I

blurted out the pregnancy, the disbelief in his eyes?

It's everything I've been terrified of these past weeks come to life at once, and it's my own damned fault for keeping this from him. I've made it worse.

"Who called the police?" Nina demands, and I turn toward her.

"I did. But everything's fine now."

"Everything's not fine!" Carter shouts, his voice reedy as he points at Jax, who's looking between his fist and my business partner, glaring at both. "He hit me with no cause whatsoever."

"Oh, there was cause." Jax's voice is deathly low, and Mace places a hand on his friend's shoulder.

"There's no problem," I insist, crossing to the officer who appears to be in charge. "I phoned to get help finding a friend of ours, and I appreciate you coming, but we've found him."

"My face is bleeding!" Carter wheezes from behind me, and I wince. "That man hit me, and I would like to press charges."

The officers survey all of us standing on the steps in our evening clothes.

"We can take statements here or down at the station," he says to Jax, who's at the bottom of the steps, fists still clenched, staring like he can't believe any of this.

"You've got to be fucking kidding me." Jax lunges for Carter again, and one of the officers steps between them as my throat tightens in shock.

"I'm sorry, Mr. Jamieson, but we're gonna have to do it this way." He's behind him, putting cuffs on my fiancé.

The sight of those cuffs spurs me into action. No matter what remains unanswered between me and Jax, no one's taking my fiancé away. "Stop it!"

But the officer marches a semi-compliant Jax down the steps. I follow, tripping in my heels and narrowly avoiding wiping out. "Jax!"

By the time I'm at the bottom, the officer's got him in the car. I pound on the back window. Jax is saying something, but I can't hear.

The officer who cuffed Jax rounds the hood of the car and holds up a hand. "Ma'am, you're going to have to step back."

"Bullshit I am."

It's one thing for Jax and I to disagree, but no one comes between us.

I whirl on my heel to take in the other officer, who's got a notepad open and is talking to Carter. "What are you doing?"

He pauses, patient. "Taking statements. If you'd prefer to give yours down at the station with Mr. Jamieson, that can be arranged."

I don't consider myself a rebel. Bucking authority has extended to my professors and Cross. I've never gone up against an armed police officer before, but I can't contain my agitation.

"You bet your ass I will," I bite out.

The second officer walks down the stairs and gets into the passenger seat of the car. I watch the vehicle pull away, panic vibrating through me.

"Haley, we still need to talk about this proposal."

Carter's voice has me taking the stairs two at a time, my ankle wobbling halfway up before I stop in front of him.

"If you want to submit it, go ahead, but those cops took Jax away in a squad car. That's what matters. It's all that matters. We'll still have a business two weeks from now, with or without this client. And I'll have to figure out how to step away for more than two weeks at a time, because when I have this baby"—his eyes widen on mine—"I'm going to have to."

Hands find my shoulders, comforting. *Serena.*

"Where's Annie?" I ask her, emotion suddenly catching up with me.

"Here."

Jax's daughter appears at the top of the stairs, eyes wide.

"Come on."

I jerk my head toward the parking lot, but by the time Annie's down the stairs, Mace already has the Bentley pulled up.

I throw him a grateful look. "I'm driving."

Mace cocks his head. "How about you take the back and let me drive, Mama Bear? There's been a lot of excitement tonight."

I shoot him a glare before rounding to the passenger seat.

Annie slides into the back, followed by Serena.

After fastening my seat belt, I pass Serena my phone because my hand is shaking. "Our lawyer's in the contacts. Can you call and tell him what happened? I don't think I can do it without swearing."

She nods. "No problem."

"Good." I twist around to meet Annie's worried gaze. "Now let's go get your dad."

"I wish I didn't have to do this, Mr. Jamieson," the police officer, who can't be older than the stripper cop from the bachelor party, apologizes as he shuts me in the cell.

I rub my wrists to erase the feeling of the metal cuffs he removed moments ago. "Makes two of us."

I don't care that he feels like shit about this. I care that I'm in a lockup cell less than forty-eight hours before my own wedding and my fiancée just announced she's pregnant with my child.

"At least it's a quiet night. No one's gonna bother you much."

Bother me? I'm behind bars with two days until the biggest moment of my life, we have no wedding venue, and my fiancée is out there somewhere with the dickhead who put me in here.

"You know I'm a huge fan."

I turn on my heel, take the three strides that carry me to the back of the cell, and lean my head against the wall, shutting my eyes.

"I have all your albums. My favorite is *Redline*." He goes quiet a minute, and I think I've been granted a reprieve.

Until he sings under his breath.

I resist the urge to grind the heels of my hands against my eyes. It's been a long time since I truly couldn't escape my reality. I like to think I'm always under pressure, but this is the first time in a long time I've felt like this.

After two full verses, the singing stops.

I crack an eye to see the cop surveying the inside of my cell. "I know it's not the greatest in here, but it could be worse."

"I've been in lockup before," I say under my breath.

"Really?"

"I was eighteen. I took food to feed my family." I remember it like yesterday. Cross showed up, gave me an ultimatum. One that changed my life.

"Well, then I'm glad."

I blink at him. "Excuse me?"

"It gave us your music. It's the way it was meant to be. You know, I wanted to be a major league pitcher," he says, conversational. "Was all-state in high school. But I saw someone get robbed at gunpoint in my neighborhood. Seeing it firsthand, I knew I wanted to do this. To make a difference."

Despite the thoughts circling my head, I can't help tuning into his words. "Few minutes later, you wouldn't have seen that. Maybe you'd be on ESPN right now instead of here."

He shakes his head, rocking on the balls of his feet. "Not how it was meant to be. The universe has a plan."

Before I can turn that over, I hear a familiar female voice come from down the hall. "I need to see him."

There's the sound of some debate, followed by footsteps.

Haley appears, her hair messy around her face, her heels clicking on the floor. The fierceness in her expression is replaced by relief when she sees me.

"Jax! Are you okay?"

"I'm fine." I'm at the bars in a heartbeat, reaching through to grab her arms. Her fingers clutch my forearms as she looks me over head to toe, breathless. "Listen, about the pregnancy—"

"Before you do, there's something else I need to say."

She reaches for my hand, presses it against her stomach. I focus on the warmth under my hand through the thin dress, try to process what she's saying even though it feels as if my brain is incapable of producing a single rational thought right now.

"I was afraid to tell you," she confesses. Those words, and the pain in her voice, stop my heart. "At first it was because of the miscarriage last time, and then I was in Philly, and that seemed like a terrible thing to say on a video call. So, I decided to wait for the right time. But then the other day, you said something about kids changing everything, not always for the better..."

I curse violently enough one of the officers coughs. "I found condoms in Annie's suitcase. I didn't say anything because I didn't want to stress you out more."

Understanding has her brows lifting, her mouth forming a little O. "That's why you were so worried about her."

I nod. "Turns out they were Kyle's."

I'm still pissed I made such a mistake, but I can't think about it because she's studying me, her eyes damp with unshed tears.

Her closeness soothes my aching chest, but the pain doesn't go away. It deepens, spreads through my gut. But with it comes another emotion, a bigger one.

"Hales, sweetheart..." My throat works. "I've always wanted kids with you. Probably since you stole my hoodie."

"You gave it to—"

"Fine. I gave you my hoodie. You stole my heart though."

Her eyes crinkle at the corners.

"And I don't give a fuck about the timing. I had it all planned out, the timing, but I can't control it. I get that. This is our future, our adventure. As long as I have you, I can do anything."

"Really?" Haley's gaze meets mine as she traces a finger down one of the bars, and I'd give all I have to melt them from between us.

My own eyes burn as a tear slips down her cheek, and I wipe it away with my thumb.

Her voice is low and soft. "I think, deep down, I knew you'd be on board. But I felt like there's been so much change these past few years that I've barely kept up. Now... it matters. With you and Annie and the baby"—my chest swells hearing her say those words—"everything matters more. I've never had much family, so I've learned to take care of myself. But this is bigger than me, and I'm afraid I'll mess it up."

I'm aching to hold her so damned much. I've never resented anything the way I'm resenting the steel between us. "You'll be a great mom. Hell, you are to Annie already. She looks up to you."

The glistening in her eyes makes me swallow my own emotion. "Besides. By all standards, I'm a terrible father. I spent ten years on the road leaving my kid with her aunt and uncle while I toured packed stadiums."

Haley's eyes widen. "You are *not* a terrible father."

I think about the condom debacle earlier. "Pretty sure Annie might say I am. Point is none of us are qualified, Hales. We do the best we can. Sometimes it's terrible. Sometimes it's pretty great."

"You're right." She sucks in a breath and holds it. "You're right about something else too—I have been working too much. Between the move and our baby, I've been throwing myself into the things I know I'm capable of. But I want to be here, Jax. I want to be in Dallas, with you. And I want to be a mom," she vows, and I think again of how damned lucky I am.

We're in the middle of a jail two nights before our wedding, but my mouth curves into a smile. "I'm scared too. But ten years from now, maybe I'll be back on a stage, or maybe I'll never pick up a guitar again. Only thing I know is I'm going to love you, Haley. Nothing could make me stop."

Her face flushes with happiness, and I feel as if a huge weight's been lifted off us both. "I'm glad we're getting married. And then I'm glad we're going to Bali so I don't have to look at unpacked boxes anymore."

"I'll have someone unpack them while we're gone," I promise, and she laughs. "But first, we need to get out of here. Is he pressing charges?" I look at the officers, but it's Haley who answers.

"No. And I told him I'm taking the next two weeks off and won't be looking at work until I get back. And your lawyer should be here..." She glances down the hall. "Now."

"Good. Because there's something I want to show you."

A throat clearing has us both looking past Haley.

The cop shifts on his feet. "Sorry to interrupt, Mr. Jamieson, but would it be all right if I got a selfie?"

15

HALEY

"Can I look?" I ask Jax.

"Not yet."

The ground bumps under us as the golf cart covers our backyard.

Yard is the wrong word. Estate, farm, small nation is more like it.

"I'm pretty sure you're taking me somewhere I've never been," I say, my fingers still over my closed eyes.

"My ego says that every time we're together."

I snort at his cocky tone.

I'm still reeling from the arrest. Seeing Jax get taken away in a police car, seeing him behind bars, sent a spike of cold through me...

chased by the conviction that I would've torn down the entire jail to get him out if I'd had to.

The idea of being separated from him was intolerable, which reminded me of a truth I'd forgotten: as long as I have Jax, I can figure anything out.

Maybe Jax felt the same, because when everyone descended on us at once when we arrived home, he silenced them, saying, "We'll talk in the morning. Go to sleep."

Now we're bumping toward God knows where at two in the morning in a golf cart.

I hadn't meant to tell Jax about my pregnancy at the rehearsal dinner—if there was a right time, it definitely wasn't that—but it tumbled out. I hadn't realized how much keeping that in had cost me until I saw his face transform at my announcement.

I've never seen him look so stunned. But the second he was released, he kissed me as if he couldn't even wait to get out of the building, hands stroking down my sides, thumbs caressing my waist with a kind of reverence I never knew I wanted.

The golf cart stops. Anticipation works

through me even before he says, "All right. You can look."

I blink my eyes open, and my chest tightens. "Jax, what did you do?"

I grip the overhead bar and shift out of the cart, my eyes locked on the huge wooden structure. The gazebo's a story and a half tall and big enough to hold a carousel.

"You said you wanted one. So, we built you one."

My hands run over the wood, smoothed and finished. The color is pale white in the moonlight, the beautiful lines and curves etching themselves into my heart. "This is..."

"Tell me you like it."

I take the three steps up, stop in the middle, and stare into the peaked roof. Then my gaze drops to the floor, the checkerboard pattern of dark and light wood reminding me of the chess games we used to play.

By the time I look back at Jax, I'm so full of wonder it's incredible I can find words. "It's the most beautiful thing I've ever seen.

"When?" I ask once I get control of myself.

He runs critical eyes over the beams and benches. "Had a little time on my hands while you were gone the last month. The guys helped."

Conviction works through me, along with acceptance and utter adoration. "It's perfect. You're perfect."

His brows lift. "Perfect, huh?" His hand finds my stomach, his thumb stroking as if he's processing what this all means. "My wife and the mother of my child said I'm perfect. Now I wish I could record it. Ahead of the times I dodge diaper duty or dress our kid wrong."

"You'll never hear it again," I tease, though I'm secretly fantasizing about the family we'll have together.

Seeing Jax with Annie already melts my ovaries. Seeing him with a baby? Our baby?

Between our new child's around-the-clock needs and my desire for him, my fiancé may never sleep again.

Jax's touch stills, then drifts south. "That's too bad. Because there's a lot I'd do to hear it."

There's no cockiness in his voice this time, only love. His hand finds me, and my breath hitches, the cool air burning my lungs contrasting with the sweet heat from his fingers.

He pulls back too soon, and I have to swallow my protest. "We shouldn't do this here. It might hurt you. Or the baby."

I bite my cheek. "The baby's fine. He or she is this big right now." I hold up my thumb and forefinger.

"So, I don't need to hold back."

I shake my head, trying not to laugh at how intent he looks. The concentration on my fiancé's face when we talk about this baby is like nothing I've ever seen.

"Not for a few months at least."

Despite my assurances, he lays me down with care on one of the benches.

We make love, and it feels like home. He feels like home.

Jax touches me reverently, stroking me into a state of need. I touch him everywhere, as if I can't get enough, because I can't.

Every time I try to speed up, he slows us down. Eventually I give up fighting it, let the overwhelming sense of rightness wash over me.

When he slips inside me, I sigh at the way he fills me, body and soul.

Finding love is easy. Keeping it, trusting it,

putting it first on the good days and the bad ones... that's what takes courage.

When we come down after the high, I'm looking up at the beautiful ceiling, marveling at the craftsmanship. "This is really the perfect place," I murmur. "It feels like home, Jax. It feels like us."

"I'm glad you think so." Jax's low voice strokes down my spine. "There's something I need to tell you, too."

I turn toward him, the hairs on my neck lifting.

"The minister called earlier tonight at the rehearsal dinner. He won't to marry us in his church."

My heart stops. "Are you kidding? Why not?"

"Apparently, our offer to replace the urn Nina defaced smoothed things over until he started receiving threatening emails from environmental groups and concerned individuals after Kyle posted his video on social media, and he won't 'bring any further wrath upon his congregation.'"

I search his face, but he looks more amused than concerned. Maybe spending a few hours in jail changed his perspective. "But how are we supposed to find a new location for a wedding on two days' notice?"

Jax shifts onto an elbow, brushing a piece of hair behind my ear. "You called this the perfect place. Who am I to argue with my wife?"

My fingers dig into his arms as I realize what he's suggesting. "That's insane," I inform him, although there's a new tingling in my chest. "Impossible. And even if it were possible? Nina would never speak to us again."

His wicked grin melts me. "Let's find out."

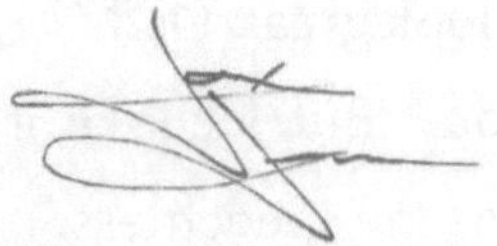

DAY OF THE WEDDING

"Jax Jamieson with stage fright. Never thought I'd see the day."

Mace grins from behind my shoulder in the floor-length mirror.

"Fuck that." I knot my tie, but my fingers are clumsy. It's an alarming feeling given I've made my living with these hands.

"We need reinforcements," he says, making for the door.

"No drinking." My commanding voice has

him stopping. "I want to remember this. Every second."

I forget the tie for the moment when I glance back toward the doorway and see a girl dressed in soft purple. Her lips curve.

"Wow. You look great, Dad."

"Back at you." But I choke it out because my daughter has me speechless.

"Don't think getting yourself arrested buys you sympathy for the condom thing," she says but crosses to me. Her fingers go to work on my tie. "I'm still pissed you tried to send Tyler away."

"Does he know why?"

She shakes her head. "And he's not going to. You and me are going to talk about this. Maybe we'll even yell. But not today." She finishes, smooths down the black satin. "Today's for you and Haley."

Sometimes her maturity blows me away.

My daughter, who used to curl up next to me to read the *Harry Potter* books I bought her. Who trusted me to teach her how to swim, who bounced in the audience next to her aunt Grace in the VIP seats at my concerts.

I turn back to the mirror as I swallow the emotion rising up. "Thanks, kid."

She blinks, her smile tightening as if she's trying to contain hers, too. "Well. I just came in to say break a leg. You'll do great."

Annie folds me in a hug, and my ribs expand to the point of cracking. Too soon, she releases me and heads for the door, squeaking as another figure appears in the hallway beyond.

"Hey," he says.

"Hi."

"You look... beautiful."

"Thank you." In the mirror, I see my kid flush, then duck past the man—boy—in the tux. "You too."

"I look beautiful?" I can just hear his low voice sounding amused.

"Yes," she decides, laughing.

"Tyler, come in," I call.

He complies.

"Shut the door. You change your mind about meeting some producers later today?"

"No."

"Good." I stare at him. "I want to help you with whatever's happening at home."

His expression clouds. "You don't even know—"

"It doesn't matter. I will help you resolve it, and then I can make you into the best musician you could ever be. Whether that's headlining arenas and flying on private jets or playing pickup for some second-rate act. They don't define you. You do that. If you're up to it."

He shakes his head, bewildered. "Why? You've done enough letting me help with Big Leap, inviting me here."

I reach for the boutonniere on a side table, white and the same shade of purple as Annie's dress.

"Consider it an investment. Someone did the same for me, and though I didn't like how he did it, I can't regret the outcome."

I pierce the fabric of the tux with the pin, adjusting the tiny flower arrangement until it's level and then meeting Tyler's gaze in the mirror.

"Before you answer, there's a condition. Few things in my life are precious to me. My family is one."

"Haley's been good to me since the day I met her," Tyler says levelly. "And Annie..." His attention drops to the carpet as he shoves his hands in his pockets. "She looks at the world like no one else. I don't know what I did before her friendship."

Satisfaction settles in my gut as I reach for his tie, tucking in the tail where it's escaped. "It should go without saying that I expect anyone in my circle to look out for my family. To never put personal interests ahead of Haley's." My jaw works. "Or Annie's."

I replay the teasing I overheard in the hallway moments ago, and from the dawning understanding on Tyler's face, he's thinking of it too.

"My daughter needs friends. She doesn't need distractions. Flirtations." The emphasis on this word isn't an accident. "Anyone who might hurt her, intentionally or not. There are enough people like that already in the world."

I think of the threat to Annie, the woman who's been lurking all week. The one my lawyer has insisted hasn't raised her head that security has on their blacklist.

"If I learn you've acted in a way that contravenes our agreement, you'll wish you'd never heard my name. Do you understand?"

Tyler glances back toward the door, still closed, and I'm surprised he's hesitating. I wonder about the emotions chasing themselves across his half-turned face.

But by the time he meets my gaze, his expression is calm. "Yes."

When we decided to move the wedding to our place, Nina arranged a tent for the food and a fleet of golf carts to move people around.

The weather has cooperated, and it's warm and sunny as I head out the back of the house to find my groomsmen standing by the golf carts.

"I don't get sentimental, but I wanna thank you. You've been with me a lot of years. Some longer than others"—I meet Mace's gaze—"but you're all brothers to me."

They nod. Mace's eyes get glassy.

"Let's get this over with," I say gruffly.

The ride down to the gazebo feels like entering another world. The trees have been decorated with white gauze, and there's a gravel path laid down with flowers on either side. When the golf cart rounds the last grove of trees, I see rows of chairs filled with people I've worked with, friends from the industry.

I'd expected people would throw a fit about the venue change, but Nina said most were fine with it.

As our golf carts pull up behind a white wall covered in flowers that was erected for the wedding, my gaze goes to the tent nearby, where the girls are getting ready.

"No peeking." Nina appears from nowhere, dressed in her purple dress.

Brick's eyes bug out of his head.

"You found a purple sling to go with the dress?" I say, impressed.

"Of course. I had it made from the same fabric." She turns to Mace with a smile. "You're up."

Mace is the only one of us who's a qualified wedding officiant, so he heads for the gazebo first, the service in his hands, and he takes up his post.

"Thank you for all of this," I say under my breath.

"For all the trouble you gave me, you were always my favorite, Jax Jamieson." Nina squeezes my arm. "Now get your ass up there."

Three steps lead into the gazebo, and I savor each of them, feeling the sturdiness under my feet as I move to stand in front of Mace. I sneak one last look at the structure we built.

Our bridal party will be taking their seats on benches lining the gazebo decorated with boughs of flowers. Our friends resting on the wood I built with my own hands. My sister Grace in the front row, smiling.

It feels right.

Grooms always look awkward as fuck, and now, as I turn to face the guests, I get it. I scan the faces, millions of dollars of fashion, but I'm barely seeing them.

When the song we chose for the processional starts, the voice is familiar. I cut a startled glance over at Lita, playing with a band in a nearby tent. She smiles, and I shake my head in appreciation.

Then I glance back down the aisle and see Brick and Nina. Next come Kyle and Annie. Finally Serena, on her own since Mace is already here.

By the time the wedding party takes their spots next to me in the gazebo, my emotions are bigger than my chest. I bow my head, so full of feeling I might explode.

Pride that these are my family and friends. Gratitude for everyone who could come.

Grief for everyone who's not here and who had a part in our story.

It's been a long journey to get here, and our journey's not over. I've packed venues around the globe. Made more millions than I could ever spend. But this—family, friends, *life*—this humbles me.

Murmurs start in the crowd.

Mace's throat clears, and I lift my chin.

Her white dress is sleeveless and dips into a V at her chest. The skirt flows out around her, behind her. Her sleek, dark hair's pulled back from her face, a simple headband of flowers atop her hair.

But it's her face that gets me.

Flushed rosy skin.

Full, pink lips.

My heart stops as Haley's gaze finds mine.

She's fifty feet away, but I swear I feel her breath, smell her skin. Dark, almond eyes lined by thick lashes and full of something it could take a lifetime to process.

I want to spend every second doing just that.

She moves toward me, Jerry at her side, her arm looped through his. I can't tell if he's holding her up or she's holding him up.

And that's the thousandth reason I love her.

It could take seconds or hours for her to reach me, and I don't care either way. It's too long to stand apart from her and not near long enough to admire her. To bask in the pride and fucking appreciation of knowing she's sharing her life with me.

When she reaches the gazebo, she turns to stand in front of me, Serena helping with her train as Jerry sits with a huff of breath on the bench. His eyes are damp.

"Friends, family, industry insiders it would have been impolite to leave out..." A chuckle goes up from the crowd before Mace continues. "We're here in this beautiful, sturdy, and well-stained gazebo today to watch Jax marry Haley."

I can't help smiling as Mace speaks. Haley beams too.

He goes through a few more remarks before asking, "Do you have the vows?"

We both nod.

Although the idea of being married in the church I went to as a child held a certain nostalgia, intimacy is more important.

The minister who kicked us out of his church might've been within his rights to do so, but the chaos was our chaos—the chaos of friends and family and people who care about one another doing the best they know how.

And the security guards at the estate were following guidelines by ignoring an elderly man stumbling past them into the dark, but any one of our crew would've stopped him immediately and done anything in their power to make sure he was safe.

When we changed the venue for both the ceremony and the reception, we'd decided to write our own vows. From the moment Haley proposed it, that felt like the easiest decision of all.

"Haley, would you like to start?"

She looks at me, her face open and beautiful and everything I could ever want.

"Jax." The love in her voice nearly brings

me to my knees. "I swore I knew you before I met you. Your words got me through the hardest times of my life. My impression was that you were someone who knew what it meant to live, how to face it all and come through the other side.

"When I got to know you, I realized I was wrong. Not that you hadn't lived, but that there was so much more to you. You're larger than life, but it's the quiet moments, the secret ones, that won me over. It's who you are as a friend. A brother. A father. I love that I get to witness it, that I see you not only when you're brilliant and brave, but when you're troubled and humble."

My throat works.

"I'm not used to having someone care about me like you do, someone who wants me to see only the best of the world. Even though we come at the world from different directions, I know you respect me and we want the same things.

"It's not enough to say that I will love you and cherish you, because that implies you're something outside of me. You're part of me, Jax. You're my today, my tomorrow, my forever.

"I love you so damn much." Her eyes tear up, and my chest expands even more, until I'm not sure how I'm not floating up to the rafters. "And everything I have, everything I am... I share it with you."

17

———

HALEY

This morning, I woke up alone in bed with a buzzing in the back of my brain. It took three seconds for me to remember why.

I'm marrying Jax Jamieson today.

I sleep-walked through getting ready, rehearsed my vows in my head.

But it didn't become real while I was putting on the beautiful dress.

Not when my hair was plaited into a crown or when my lips were lined and painted.

Not when I walked down that aisle, my legs steadier than I expected.

Not even when I caught sight of my husband, looking like the most breathtaking thing I'd ever seen in his perfectly tailored black tux.

It was when I stopped in front of Jax, his amber gaze stealing from and giving to me at once. That look blasted away any remnants of uncertainty from the past week—about our future, about me, about all of it.

This is what I want.

I recite the vows I spent the last two days writing and rewriting because I wanted them to be right.

Eventually I decided it was more important that they were real.

Like us.

My throat bobs as I finish. Judging by the adoration on Jax's face, the way his eyes glisten as he stares at me like I'm the only other person on the planet...

It worked.

"I have to kiss you right now," Jax murmurs so only we can hear, his fingers threading between mine, his thumb stroking my palm.

"So, do it," I whisper back.

"Um. Guys?" This from Mace. "That's supposed to be later."

"You're not even a real minister," Jax gripes.

"Come on, man. Help me out a little."

Jax clears his throat.

He has me from the first word.

"Hales, I'm not patient. I'm not forgiving. I'm suspicious. I don't give people the benefit of the doubt.

"But having a family, including you, has changed everything. Each day is brighter because you're in it. Each night is less dark with you at my side. I can't promise to be patient. I can't promise I'll be forgiving. But I will be really fucking grateful each time you give me another chance.

"Because my heart is full of you."

My lips tremble at the honesty in his voice.

"When you're not beside me, I'll wish you were. When you're threatened, I will hunt your demons. When you're filled with joy, I will give thanks for the privilege of seeing you smile."

I swallow.

"In this lifetime and all lifetimes after it...

"You are mine. Not because you give yourself to me. But because I give myself to you."

My gaze drops to his tux, where the tattoo sits over his chest, and he taps it.

God, I love this man. Five years ago, I

couldn't have imagined this being my life. Meeting Jax Jamieson. Falling for him. Having the man I thought I knew turn out to be even better.

Every part of our journey was important and needed. Even the hardest parts. Especially the hardest parts.

We manage to get through the exchange of rings, my heart hammering as I slide the band onto his finger.

When we're finished, I cut a look at Mace. "We good?"

"Yeah. I pronounce you…"

But we're already kissing.

And everyone's already shouting.

And life is beautiful.

After the ceremony, we sign the register.

I have a few surprises for my new husband, and I can't wait to share them with him.

When the music resumes, we both look over at the tent. Annie's at the microphone, singing with Lita, her voice smooth and bright.

My gaze flicks between Annie and Tyler,

who's standing with his guitar a few feet away. "You're not still worried about them, are you?"

His jaw works as his hand finds my shoulder, brushing across the skin there. "Not anymore."

Before I can ask what he means, Jerry pipes up, "Is it time for food?"

"Sure thing, Jerry," Nina says. "We'll do some pictures, then catering will be set up in that tent."

"And a bar," he says.

"The bar is already set up."

Jerry's eyes gleam.

Jax, the wedding party, and I take photos at the gazebo, in front of the house, and by the pool.

We even take some funny ones on the Big Leap bus, the girls pretending to play guitars while the guys watched on longingly.

"Smile, Jax," the photographer says. "But try not to look too smug."

"You know how much I get paid to pose in photos?" my husband gripes. "Think I know when I'm smug."

"You are," our photographer replies.

I laugh, and Jax cuts me a wry look that turns into something deeper, lingering.

When photos are done, we join the others in the tent where staff are circulating with hors d'oeuvres. Then we take our seats, and the speeches begin, but even though the food's delicious, I can't finish anything.

"You gotta eat, Hales," Jax says. "There're two of you in there."

"We're both too excited." My gaze scans the room and the round tables before it lands on one figure in the back. "You broke Carter's nose, you know."

"It was worth it."

I bite my cheek to hold in a smile. "It was a bit uncharitable of you considering he helped me out with something important. Your wedding gift," I go on at his perplexed look.

"What are you talking about?"

"Part of the work I did when I was in Philly was lobbying funding groups about the expansion to Big Leap." I chew my lip. "I was playing phone tag this week because I wanted to make sure it was finalized in time."

Jax's lips part, and the shock on his face is the best possible reward. "You didn't."

I grin. "It's almost as much as what we missed out on last time. Carter was able to use some of his university connections to get me an introduction I needed."

"I could introduce you wherever you want."

"Yes, but that would have ruined the surprise," I point out, and Jax pulls me to him for a kiss that's softer than I expect.

"I didn't think you could give me a better gift," he murmurs when he pulls back, his gaze dropping to my stomach. "But that's pretty damn good too. I guess I'll be back at Big Leap once we return from our honeymoon."

"That's good news. It'll make a lot of kids ecstatic to be able to work with you." I survey the crowd around us, table after table of beautiful people and famous faces. I lower my voice. "That show at Grenada, Jax... that was something else. You ever think of making a comeback? I hear babies are a lot of work, but there're two of us. Eventually, you'll have time again."

I expect him to say, "Hell no," but he's quiet, which in itself is telling.

"I'm thinking about how you convinced me

to return to the industry last time," he murmurs at my raised eyebrow.

The memory of dropping to my knees in front of the man I hadn't seen in two years but couldn't stop loving is one I'll never forget.

"I almost couldn't stop," I admit, and his eyes flash with hunger and smugness.

"You don't ever have to stop again."

God, I wish we were alone right now.

I have to force myself to focus when Nina says it's time to reveal the cake.

I gape in astonishment at the white monstrosity. It's five layers of ice-smooth fondant, buttercream flowers, and ribbons draped artfully around each tier. And on top...

Jax lifts the cake topper to inspect it, a chuckle rocking his shoulders.

There's a tiny groom in a tux with a guitar slung over his back. A bride is kissing him, one foot popped in the air with a tiny Converse sneaker peeking out from under her dress.

"You didn't," he says.

I lift the hem of my dress, revealing a pair of white high-tops I dug out of one of the boxes from Philly. "I wore heels for the ceremony, but

I figured this could be my something old. In honor of our beginnings."

Jax grins, shaking his head.

"You didn't do the whole rhyme thing, did you?" His brow furrows.

"Well, the whole dress is new, and I borrowed this from Rena"—I point to a clip in my hair—"so I figured I was halfway there. And as for blue…"

"You're not wearing blue," he says without breaking my gaze. "I would've noticed."

My lips brush his ear as I lower my voice. "You haven't seen what's under the dress."

His eyes darken. "Fuck, I love you."

I laugh as we cut the cake, then Jax tugs me out to the dance floor.

Our friends join us. Wes and Serena, whom I definitely heard making up this morning in their room and who now look happier than ever. Nina and Brick. Kyle and… some woman from a reality TV series. I search for Annie and Tyler, but Annie's talking to Lita.

I gesture with my chin, and Tyler comes over. "You're not going to dance?"

"I don't dance," he says.

"Of course not," I agree, serious.

Jax's lips brush my jaw as we sway together.

"We survived our wedding, and we're six months from being parents. You trying to start trouble?"

"I don't cause trouble. I'm a happily married woman whose husband pledged to love, honor, and obey her."

"That's not exactly what I said."

"Mmm, it's what I heard."

Jax pulls back, his eyes twinkling. "I think I'm gonna like forever with you."

My heart swells until it's threatening to escape my ribs. "Me too."

EPILOGUE

ONE WEEK LATER

"I swear you're clean."

"But I can still feel it." Haley spreads her toes wide, frowning.

I laugh under my breath. "You know, the feeling of sand between your toes is supposed to be a good thing. Some people call it orgasmic."

"I call it itchy. Don't get me wrong, I liked the snorkeling and lying on the beach this morning. It's the leftover sand that's a problem. Feels like little animals creeping over my skin."

"Little animals, huh?"

My fingers find the sole of her foot, and her hazel gaze locks on mine. "Don't you dare."

I stroke my thumb along the bottom of her foot, and she shrieks. My grip on her ankle keeps her from scrambling away.

"No one's gonna hear you, Hales." I glance around the green-blue water surrounding our private hut at the end of the pier.

We've been here for three days, and I'm already feeling the most right I have in years. More than when I left tour or got custody of my kid. Haley is too—the shadows under her eyes are gone, and she's more playful, more present. This honeymoon cost a small fortune since we wanted an entire expanse of the island to ourselves with no one else in sight, but I'd pay twice that to know Haley's happy.

"Housekeeping won't come until tomorrow. So, you're at my mercy," I say.

"Mercy is not something you're known for."

"Lucky for you, I'm less interested in your feet and more interested in the rest of you." My gaze runs down her body, clothed in a black bikini top that fastens at the center with a gold clasp and matching sarong I picked out. I shift over her, my loose short-sleeved button-down fluttering in the sea breeze.

"I want to see it."

"Yeah?" Pleasure floods me.

I rock back on my knees, trying for patience as she unbuttons my shirt. Her breath catches as she takes in the expanse of ink on my chest, gaze lingering on the words over my heart where I had my talented tattoo artist expand the tattoo to include a T for "Telfer," which she decided to hyphenate.

I'm good with it now. I know she's mine in every way that counts.

"Good luck getting rid of me now." The teasing in her voice has me hardening in my printed shorts.

"I tried to forget you once. It didn't go so well."

Her smile broadens. "Now who's at whose mercy?"

"Maybe you need a reminder you're mine."

I reach for the mango left over from lunch and lick the chocolate dip on the end. My other hand flicks the clasp at the center of her bathing suit, and the fabric falls away, revealing her breasts.

Her mouth forms an O. "What are you doing?"

"Staking my claim."

The half-melted chocolate makes a perfect crayon as I draw on her breast. Haley laughs until I run the fruit over her pebbled nipple. Arousal clouds the humor on her face until she's arching her neck.

I get a J and an A before the chocolate's mostly gone. It takes hard work to get the third letter, both on account of the fruit and the fact that I'm so fucking turned on by having her breasts bared to me and the sun, her hips pinned between my legs, her stomach that I swear is starting to curve in a way that's so fascinating it's hard to look away from.

Haley glances at her chest, lip caught between her teeth. "It looks like a T. Who's Jat? Is he cute?"

I stare at my wife.

There's no woman I could possibly adore more.

I kiss her, sink into her. With my body, I show her what she means to me in a way no marks on flesh ever could. What we have is sweeter than words, deeper than ink, more solemn than vows.

I touch her everywhere except where I wrote my name. That will stay pristine for as long as I can manage it.

And when I sink inside her, pin her hands over her head and thrust long and slow in that way that makes her eyes change color, I know I must have done something right.

Because this is it. This is everything.

We're everything.

And no matter what happens at home, with our family, with work, we've got this covered.

It's hours later when I sit up in bed—a heavenly mattress on the floor of the hut. The sun's already setting when Haley's phone rings.

She groans. "I swear I turned that off."

"I'll do it," I say, reaching past her to the nightstand and opening the drawer. I look at the number and laugh.

Haley's eyes widen when she can tell I'm going to answer her phone. "What are you doing? We said no phones this week."

"I know, but give me this one." I hit Accept and shift back against the wall. "Connor."

"Jax." Irritation and surprise come down

the line from continents away, the beauty of modern technology. "I need to talk to Haley."

My wife shakes her head, which gives me immense satisfaction.

I grin. "Yeah, I don't think so. We're on our honeymoon. You know what that means?"

"I don't need—"

"It means we're enjoying ourselves. Being married isn't the same as dating. It takes a lot of compromise. Making sure everyone gets what they want. Which means lots and lots of practice."

Haley digs a toe into my side, and I grab for her foot. This time she's too fast and yanks it away.

"Listen. I wanted to tell her that the bid I finished? Well, we got the project."

"I'm sure she'll be delighted to hear it," I say.

Silence hangs over the line, the only sounds coming from the ocean licking at the moorings outside the hut.

Haley's sitting up now, but she seems content to let me have my fun. My gaze roams her skin, flushed from hours of sex, the smudges of chocolate illegible across her breasts.

"She tell you we got matching tattoos?" I ask.

Haley rolls her eyes, dropping back against the bed as she mutters something that sounds like, "How old are you?"

"Uh. No. She didn't." He clears his throat. "Just tell her I called."

"I won't," I say. "Bye, Connor."

"It's—"

I click off, toss the phone back into the drawer, and stretch.

My wife looks at me with amusement. "You ever going to stop giving him a hard time?"

"Never. You might work with him, but he needs to be reminded I won the prize."

"I'm not a prize." But her tone is light as she shifts out of bed, motioning me with a finger to follow.

I do, straightening next to her. "Yeah, you are. You're what I fought for every day. I just didn't know it."

Her eyes shine. "I love you, you know that?"

"I love you too, Hales." I follow her out of the hut to the outdoor shower.

She steps under the spray, and I take a minute to admire her before joining her.

"I'm starting to think we should never go home," I say.

The cool water doesn't do much for my hot skin when I rub body wash over her ass, tugging her against me. She starts to wash the chocolate off her breasts, and I remove her hands, doing it instead with a hint of regret as the last traces wash away.

"We have some exciting things on the horizon. A new home in Dallas. Big Leap expanding. New projects for me to work on, whenever I have time for them because..." She rubs a hand over her stomach, and my face splits into a grin.

I soap up her stomach even more carefully than her breasts.

"Annie thinks it's a girl."

"It's definitely a boy."

Haley's brows shoot up. "Don't tell me you'll be disappointed if it's a girl."

I kneel and press my mouth to her navel. "Never." I peer up at her. "But girls take more protecting."

She shoves at my shoulder, and I get hit in

the face with water. "Bullshit. That's sexist. Women are as independent as guys."

"That's even worse. Independent women? Yeah, guys fall hard for independent women."

She rolls her eyes.

"The future is bright, Hales. And it's all you and me."

EPILOGUE
ANNIE

NIGHT OF THE WEDDING

"What are you doing here?"

My head snaps up at the voice emerging from the darkness, carrying over the music from the tent across the lawn. Once I recognize the silhouette approaching the gazebo, my shoulders unknot.

"Everyone's back there getting drunk," Tyler continues, taking the steps one at a time.

I lift my chin. "Most guys I know would've

snuck off with a bottle of champagne and a bridesmaid by now."

The fairy lights tucked into the rafters of the gazebo cast the strong planes of my friend's nose and cheeks in a warm glow, the hazel eyes I know as well as my own receding into shadow. His shoulders appear broader than normal in the suit, his hair tame compared to its usual wild mess.

"Maybe that's my plan." Tyler grins at me.

I roll my eyes, nodding to his empty hands. "You forgot the champagne, genius."

"Have you tried champagne? It's disgusting. I had to give it to Mace to finish because apparently it's two thousand dollars a bottle and I refused to let them throw it out."

Strains of music drift from the tent, an entire glowing world lit from the inside. Today was warm, but the breeze plays with the hairs on the back of my neck under my pinned-up hair.

I've never been in a wedding before, and between the dress and the hair, I kind of feel like a fairy princess.

Tyler could pass for a prince. He leans against the pillar, hands in the pockets of the suit that should be awkward on the boy I've seen win a hot dog eating contest.

Instead, he looks elegant.

The moment I spotted him after I finished dressing myself, staring in the mirror while a stylist braided my hair and applied more makeup than I usually wore, my chest seemed to tighten. But it was only the first surprise today, not the last.

I lift the hem of my gauzy dress and step into one of the dark squares at the edge of the chess board.

"White queen." I look up, and Tyler nods at my feet. "That's the starting position for the white queen."

"Or the black king."

"No."

"You don't think I could be a king?" I challenge him, jutting my jaw.

"Chess mimics life. The king hides in his castle. The queen goes everywhere. Does everything. She's the one who's powerful."

His casual observation might have startled the average person, but that's Tyler. He notices things others don't. The wheels behind his hazel eyes never stop turning.

"I saw you cry when Jax and Haley exchanged vows," he says, and I cock my head. "Most girls try to hide their emotions or put on what they think others expect."

I close my eyes as the music changes to a waltz. "Whoever decided tears make us weak doesn't cry enough."

"Spoken like someone who's strong to begin with."

I step forward one square. My skirt whispers against the wood, grazing the boundaries between light and dark.

I think of the woman in the catering tent with urgent eyes and skin and hair like mine who tugged me aside when I went to investigate the desserts in between speeches. The letter she pressed into my hand before I could think to stop her. The one that's now tucked into my dress.

When I look up, Tyler's prowling the opposite row of squares.

"We must be rivals, then," I tell him.

"Impossible." He cocks his head. "We'll never be on opposite sides, you and me."

I close my eyes, fall into the banter that's always been as easy as breathing with him.

"Because I know all your secrets?"

I start to take another step forward but hit a hard wall. My breath catches as I blink, tilting my chin up as I'm confronted with his handsome face.

Somehow, he's crossed the floor without making a sound.

"Not all of them."

As his dark eyes warm on mine, I realize that if I stretched onto my toes, I could smell his shampoo.

I wonder if he can smell mine.

It's a weird thought but makes perfect sense given that for all the time we've spent together, I can count on one hand the number of times we've been this close.

I've tried to place exactly what attracted me to him two years ago and decided it was our shared love of music.

But that answer satisfied me.

I think it's something bigger. Some part of us that doesn't quite fit with the world. A lock to some dark box inside us both that no key can open.

"What are you thinking?" he asks.

"That I don't like secrets." I take one step

back.

He follows me, and I suck in a startled breath as his feet move soundlessly in step with mine. "Answers aren't what they're cracked up to be. Sometimes the truth has teeth."

"It's always better to know." I take in his profile, edged by the soft fairy lights draped around the gazebo.

"Fine. You want the truth?"

The solemn expression on his face almost fools me into believing he has the truth. My truth, the one that lies somewhere between the letter in my dress and the man I've called my father for years.

I nod.

"The truth is that cake wasn't nearly as good as your Rice Krispies squares, grape smoke be damned."

"It was lavender chiffon," I retort, and he grins.

The smile transforms his face, the seriousness falling away in favor a boyish charm that's even more irresistible.

Still, it's the way my heart kicks in my chest in response that's most unnerving.

I remember my dad's mistake this week, thinking Tyler and I were having sex.

It's ridiculous.

Not the idea that I could be sleeping with someone, because I know lots of girls who are.

But that me and Tyler...

I swallow.

It's not like the guy's hard on the eyes. But in two years, Tyler and I haven't so much as kissed.

Not only has he never flirted with me, he's never checked me out. Not when we're trying to one-up each other with the latest bands or on the mission he insisted on accompanying me on to find the best veggie burger in Philly last summer. Not when we take turns doing impressions of Kyle on the drums at Big Leap or when we complain about the preppy kids at our school.

Have I wondered what it would be like to be on the receiving end of that attention?

Sure.

Any girl would.

"I ate way too much, actually," I admit, realizing he's still staring down at me. "I'm feeling kind of nauseous."

I start to turn away, but he catches my hand. The feel of his skin on mine sends little jolts of electricity up my arm.

"Careful. I don't want to ralph on your tux," I warn, my voice wavering at the edges.

"Do it. It's a rental. I've had worse nights than a pretty girl vomiting on me." His mouth twitches, but it's his words that stop my heart.

"You called me pretty," I blurt.

He stiffens for a moment, glancing back toward the tent.

Then back to me as if deciding something. "Must be the champagne."

But his words have my hands reaching for his shoulders.

I wait for him to pull away, but after a moment, his hands find my waist.

He shakes his head, sending hair falling across his lean face. "I'm gonna miss you this summer. Especially your baking."

"Rice Krispies squares don't count as baking," I inform him for the millionth time. "There's no oven involved. Besides, there must be girls at school who'd be thrilled to make you food and do your laundry, tune your guitar, anything else you might need."

"Sure."

A seed of jealousy takes up residence in my stomach until he says, "But all they see is good looks and a musician and they're useless."

"You're not that good-looking," I lie, and his face splits into a grin.

"God, yes. That's why I like you."

Tyler starts to step back, and my body protests...

He doesn't let me go. If anything, he pulls me closer as I move with him.

I bite my cheek as my pulse kicks in my chest, a beat far more powerful than the one emanating from the tent.

His touch heats at my waist, and I want to press against his hands.

"I thought you didn't dance?" I'm afraid to point it out in case this moment shatters like one of the hundreds of crystal champagne flutes stacked next to the bar.

"I don't."

Those two words have my blood humming in my veins.

I've always been good with experiencing emotions. If you name them, you stand a better chance of hanging on to them, of understanding them. But this one's hard to pinpoint.

Anticipation. Curiosity. Longing.

Possibility.

He moves us over one step. Forward. Back.

Each step has me losing track of the squares, of everything that's not him. The feel of his body.

The way his company lifts me out of the dark place I was in moments ago.

"I'm leaving tomorrow," Tyler says, and those words cool the blood in my veins.

"Don't go." The word's out before I can stop it, and I swear his fingers flex, nudging me closer. When I speak again, I'm murmuring against the lapel of his tux, the wool brushing my lips. "I got used to seeing you in the summers. Hanging out. Jamming in the Big Leap bus."

"Yeah. Me too." His exhale is heavy, as if he's considering not only leaving me but the memories too. "You've got my number."

My stomach twists, and it has nothing to do with the food. "You know it's not the same. I can't listen to a new song you're working on. Or invite you over for dinner. Or save your ass in

English when you need to write an essay on the theme of... I don't know... *King Lear* or something."

I have to tilt my chin up to meet his gaze, and my breath sticks in my throat at how near he is. I expect him to make a joke, but all he says is, "I know."

He lowers his forehead to mine, and I stop breathing.

I can definitely smell him now. Clean and masculine and a little bit woodsy. I wonder if he tastes like he smells or if he's lighter or darker. Sweeter or more bitter.

I've never wanted an answer so badly.

"It'll be a while before we see each other again," I say, struggling to keep my words from sounding choked.

"Maybe not."

His eyelids fall to half-mast, and my fingers brush through the hair above the collar of his suit. It takes everything in me not to tug him closer.

I don't know if it's him moving me anymore or the music moving both of us. I've stopped caring.

"Hey, Annie." Tyler's voice is a whisper over

my cheeks, my lips, my bare shoulders. "Promise me something."

"What's that?"

I'm aware of every part of him, from his gorgeous face to his broad shoulders and chest to his hands, fingers calloused from countless hours on the guitar.

My hands tighten around his neck. The feel of him this close has me hot everywhere despite the cool breeze.

"Don't hate me."

Confusion drags my brows together. "I could never—"

"No matter what," he interrupts. "I've got your back. Always."

Tyler's lips graze the corner of my mouth, and the lightest brush electrifies me, sends shockwaves that leave my lips and breasts and toes tingling.

But before I can respond, he's gone, down the steps and halfway across the grass toward the tent.

My fingers flex on my skirt, missing the feel of him already as I watch him disappear into the darkness.

"It'll be a while before we see each other again."

"Maybe not."

I look down and realize my feet are on the black square on the opposite side of the board.

And between the letter in my pocket and the boy who's left me tingling...

I know something is about to change.

Thank you so much for reading *Forever Wicked*! If you're not ready to let go of these characters...

Join my VIP List for an EXCLUSIVE Jax and Haley epilogue anniversary chapter! https://claims.prolificworks.com/free/ XnsF5IyN

Tyler and Annie are every bit as angsty, twisty, forbidden, thrilling, and addictive as Jax and Haley. Start reading their story now!

Read a short excerpt below

CHAPTER ONE
Annie

I hate Tyler Adams. Hating him would be my religion if music wasn't.

But he's here, facing me, his hair falling across the pillow in a dark cascade. His eyelashes are thick and so long it's unfair. His mouth is parted in sleep, the top bow firm and the bottom lush.

I'm freaking out, my heart racing a mile a minute.

He's warm. His heat emanates from his body, inviting me closer.

I hate how much I want to.

I want. I want. I want.

My thighs press together because if there's a response to that realization that doesn't involve a rush of heat flowing south, I don't know what it is.

Of course I'd never let him know that when he's awake, but he's not.

Thank God he's not.

I shift in bed, wincing as my muscles ache.

Perfect.

There's a reason I've never had sex, and if I were going to, he's the last guy I'd sleep with.

He could have so much more than this stupid place, this stupid school... Instead he sold me out for a bunch of dumb, rich assholes.

Tyler groans, and my heart leaps.

When he shifts, rolling onto his back and exposing even more beautifully carved torso, the covers ride low on his hips.

Not quite low enough to see if he's wearing anything. I swallow.

I could look.

Don't fucking look.

I press my hands to my eyes as if it'll erase the image of the beautiful guy next to me.

Two days ago, all I cared about was being on stage, impressing my rock-star father, and not falling for Oakwood Prep's rebel prince, Tyler Adams.

But when his eyes start to open…

I know I'm well and truly screwed.

TWO DAYS EARLIER

"Are you going to fuck it or just fantasize about it all day?"

The syrupy sweet voice makes me cut off my chorus halfway through a line.

"Your spoon." The platinum blonde in the front row crosses one tan leg over the other, making her plaid skirt ride up. "You're staring at it like you want to—"

"She's a mermaid, Carly. She wants to be human. It's an emotional moment." My hand tightens on the flatware from the school dining hall.

"Whatever, Little Virgin Annie. And you?" Carly turns to the corner of the stage, where Jenna's reading her lines behind a curtain of straight, dark hair. "You're wearing a garbage bag for a tail. You look homeless."

"Annie made it," Jenna blurts, turning pale under her freckles. "I was afraid I'd trip when we got our costumes, so I wanted to practice first."

I step between them. "First off, Jenna? Daniel Craig slept on park benches and J. Lo couch surfed at our age, so that's a compliment." She finds a nervous smile before I turn back to Carly. "Second, Jenna has conditional acceptance to Stanford, and your fast track is to *Real Housewives*, but that's no reason to be jealous."

Our school's queen bee edges forward in her seat. "I don't know why you're even rehearsing, Annie. Being a dumb teenager who'll never be what her daddy wants must be super relatable. I bet every night the great Jax Jamieson wishes he hadn't fucked that groupie and ended up with you."

I could beat Carly over the head with this spoon. Not hard enough to do permanent damage—assuming there are cells inside to damage—but hard enough to mess up her perfect waves. Maybe hard enough the made-up minions on either side of her would lift their overtweezed brows in surprise.

But I won't let her see her words get under my skin.

"Girls, I hope you've been practicing while I've been gone." Miss Norelli strides through the auditorium doors, returning from checking on a burnt-out stage light.

Our drama director shuffles up the aisle, her black sheath dress hugging her full figure, and takes a seat a few rows behind Carly and the others.

She pushes her purple glasses up her nose expectantly, eyes narrowed on the stage.

When the music starts again, I will myself to focus on my performance. To be a mermaid far away from the catty comments of bitchy schoolgirls who wouldn't have the first idea what to do with themselves if they ran out of people to torture.

But when I see Carly unscrew the top of my water and tip a tiny brown bottle to pour something inside, my voice wavers.

"Stop! Annie, I thought we had this section," Miss Norelli calls from her seat a few rows back.

Frustration flows through me. "We do. We did."

"Why don't we try it with the understudy?" Carly smiles as if the idea just popped into her head.

"Good idea." Norelli folds her arms, and I swallow the anger as I trade places with Carly, who holds out her hand expectantly.

I shove the spoon into her hand before flipping her off. "Wash it when you're done."

I step out of my garbage bag and retrieve my water bottle, sniffing it before shoving the thing back in my bag.

"That part never should've been yours," Lana, one of Carly's minions, whispers. "The only reason Norelli picked you is because your dad's a rock star. There's no way you got his talent."

"Carly's still the understudy," Tara, the other minion, points out. "A lot can happen in five weeks."

"Shut it, Flotsam and Jetsam." They should've been Ursula's eels, not Ariel's sisters.

Watching Carly perform, I wish she sucked, but she's actually good.

"That's enough rehearsal today," Miss Norelli says when Carly finishes. "Annie, a moment."

I get up and cross to her seat.

"Where's the girl from auditions? The fearless one, the focused one."

I shake my head. "She's here. I swear."

She sighs. "We're running out of time."

It was my decision to audition for the lead in the school musical and cross our school's reigning queen, but what even Carly doesn't know—what she can't know—is how much I need this role.

This year, everything is going to change for me. I feel it the way you feel spring in the air before anything blooms.

I cling to that conviction as I head to the front of the auditorium to pack up my things.

"Hey, princess."

I glance up to see Kellan Albright, a senior, standing over me. With his perfect dirty-blond hair and bright-white smile, he's athletic and has a decent voice. It's a curse for the rest of us because he landed the male lead and begged out of almost half of rehearsals for sports.

Of course, if any of the girls missed that many rehearsals, we'd get cut. But it's hard to find guys who're both willing and capable of doing the part.

"Look forward to seeing you at the party this weekend."

"The mid-production cast party? Canceled," Jenna offers with a look toward Carly and her minions. "Carly's solarium is getting renovated, and her parents won't have people over until it's finished."

"What about your place?" Kellan's blue eyes dance.

If looks could melt skin, mine would be peeling off from the evil stares of Carly and her minions, and I swallow an incredulous laugh. "As much as we're all BFFs, that's as appealing as waxing my eyebrows off."

He laughs as I head for the doors, falling into step next to me.

"I know I've been busy with practice, but we should rehearse together. Maybe at the party." He squeezes my arm before holding the door for me.

"Maybe."

I pass him and head to my locker to grab my books and sunglasses, the feel of his touch lingering on my bare skin.

Kellan's attractive, and a lot of girls would love his attention, but he's not my type. He's sports and parties and being seen. But right now, I'll take my allies where I can get them.

I pull out a pen and lift the front hem of my skirt to write a single word on my thigh in blue ink, then I shut my locker and head for the main doors.

If I'd thought Oakwood Prep would be simpler than the public school I attended most of my childhood, I was wrong. It's full of people with too much money and too many expectations and too many liposuction.

If I could go back to public school, go back to being normal... I'd take it in a hot second.

Because the difference between them and me is I grew up with less than nothing until I was plucked from that existence and told I was meant for another one.

Outside, I slide my sunglasses on as I head for the parking lot.

The campus is sprawling and beautiful. I soak in the spring day, the expanse of green grass, the mature trees. It's hot for Dallas, and all I want is to get home and jump in the pool.

I reach the modern steel fountain that marks the middle of the quad, the halfway point between the school and the parking lot, when a familiar form blocks my way.

I swear I've hit my daily quota of assholes.

"There are consequences for taking things that don't belong to you."

Carly stands between me and the parking lot, flanked by minions.

"Roles don't belong to people."

"I was talking about Kellan," she retorts.

"People definitely don't belong to people."

My focus falls to Lana's dirty manicure, the black smudges up her arm that weren't there during rehearsal.

Oakwood Prep is like society—the rules supposedly apply equally to everyone. They don't. Not even close.

Even amongst the rich, there are circles of power, of influence.

Carly's dad is the head of the school's board, which means she can do what she wants. To whomever she wants.

"If Kellan's your pathetic attempt not to die a virgin, good luck with that," she goes on, leaning in as she senses the kill. "No guy at Oakwood will touch you."

I close the distance between us and meet

her predatory gaze head-on. "Promise I can get that in writing?"

"Carly."

A low, smooth voice at my back has the baby hairs on my neck lifting. The minions' attention snaps to behind me.

Uniforms are an attempt to make everyone look the same. In this case, they come up short. All three guys coming down the stairs toward us are good looking, but one stands out. You'd feel this guy's magnetism in a blackout.

He's tall, with ropy arms his navy jacket can't hide, and broad enough he could carry the entire school's baggage without breaking a sweat. He has an angled jaw and cheekbones, brown eyes a little too serious to be kind, and dark, wild hair.

If Kellan is this school's preppy king, Tyler Adams is its rebel prince. He has the easy grace earned by being a senior, gorgeous, and a musician.

When he speaks, everyone listens.

When he plays the guitar, everyone worships.

"Tyler," Carly breathes. "Wanna give me a ride home?"

I don't wait around for the answer but use the distraction to dodge all of them and head to my car.

I want to get the hell out of this toxic place before I burn it down.

I shift into my silver Audi, turning the key in the ignition.

It doesn't start.

My forehead falls to the steering wheel as I remember the minions' black-streaked arms. They probably rummaged under the hood for the shiniest parts to stab at with their manicure sets.

"*The Little Mermaid*. A girl who has everything but it's still not enough."

My attention snaps toward the guy leaning in the passenger window, and I immediately regret leaving it down.

If Tyler Adams and my co-star Kellan share top billing on the "senior boys every junior girl would give their BMW to bang" list, it's for different reasons.

Kellan's full of charm, the golden boy who comes from money and radiates ease and promises of good times.

Tyler's gorgeous. Talented. Mysterious. He

comes from nothing and doesn't blink before taking everything.

But no matter how fascinating he is, it's a lie.

"Being the daughter of a king doesn't mean her life is perfect," I answer at last. "If you think so, you're dumber than you look."

He rubs a hand through his dark hair, the chunk of blue at the front that sets him apart. "But you told me I had a great future. You put on a scarf and held my hand and ogled my fate line."

"It was a charity carnival. I was fourteen."

"I paid five bucks for that spiritual advice. Don't tell me I wasted it."

I hit the start button once more. It makes a grinding noise until I slap a hand against the dash.

Please, don't let me be stranded at school.

When I blink my eyes open, Tyler's nodding through the windshield, rolling up the sleeves of his dress shirt, the jacket already gone.

I don't want Tyler Adams under my hood. But if I have to call my dad, it'll invite questions as to why my almost-new car won't start.

So, I pop the hood before rounding to the trunk for my toolkit, dropping it at his feet after I find it. Tyler yanks off his loosened tie and holds it out.

I take the tie from him, draping it around my neck for safekeeping.

I don't notice his height, his hard body, the careless way he rubs a hand over his neck as he surveys what's under my hood with a relentless intensity.

"You know why Carly fucks with you."

I shift against the front fender, twisting one end of his tie around my fingers as I watch. "She's jealous of my fashion sense."

He spares me an incredulous look. "You bait her. You walk around this place with your heart on your sleeve, begging to bleed. It's impossible for her to resist."

You could teach an AP course on making me bleed.

I knot the bottom of my shirt up around my navel to get relief from the heat. "She can't handle anyone having anything that could be hers—including the stage."

"The spotlight's not all its cracked up to be. Fans don't want you, they want what they think you possess. And the more you possess, the more people feel entitled to take."

The edge in his words catches me off guard.

I work a coiled elastic off my wrist, twisting my long hair up in a messy knot and fanning my sweat-damp neck. "Careful, Tyler. Someone might think being Prince of Oakwood is getting old."

Tyler shifts to stand in front of me in a heartbeat.

He's in my space, tall and built and intent, the weight of his attention moving from the car to me. The crisp white shirt, rolled at the sleeves, makes him look gorgeous and a little reckless, like some pirate on a mission to charm and destroy.

But it's the expression on his face, that knowing smirk, that pins me in place. It's as if he just caught me doing something filthy.

"Careful, Annie. Someone might think you give a shit."

Once, I held his hand and told his fortune.

Never again.

He betrayed me. Hurt me more than Carly's teasing and pranks ever could.

I want him to back the fuck up, but I can't

speak. Right now, all I can do is take in Tyler's light cedar scent, his half-lowered lashes, his voice a soft murmur on my skin.

I clear my throat, arch a brow. "Do you need something?"

"Yeah, I do."

Finally, he moves.

Down my body.

My breath hitches as his face is level with my chest, my waist.

I press my thighs together when his face passes my bare legs.

The heart is supposed to propel blood to your vital organs.

Mine's a traitor. It doesn't give a fuck if I live or die.

When he's this close, it beats for him.

He drops his wrench in the toolkit at my feet, and I shut my eyes in humiliated relief.

Get a grip.

If he ever finds out how I feel, the last of my pride and self-respect will go up in flames.

"What's this? Don't tell me you cheated on our English test." Tyler lifts the edge of my skirt, and I smack his hand away.

"What's under my skirt is none of your business."

He huffs out a breath as he straightens and returns to work.

"There it is," he murmurs moments later under the hood. "They yanked the coupling for your... never mind," he says at my blank expression. "Carly's better at politics than cars."

He lowers the hood, wiping the rolled-up arm of his dress shirt on his forehead. "You should be fine. If it gives you any grief, let me know."

"Thanks." The word sticks in my throat, and he holds my gaze for a beat, two.

I hurry to slide in through the driver's door. When I hit the start button, the engine roars to life.

Relief washes over me as I stuff my blazer in the back seat and unbutton my shirt another button while the A/C kicks in. Sweat beads on my chest, and I'm fastening my seatbelt when Tyler leans his muscled forearms on the driver's door.

"You get slapped with community service?" He nods toward the black garbage bag on top of my books.

I shift my sunglasses up on my head. "Oh, I led the litter pickup for Young Environmentalists at the park last week, but no, that's my practice costume for the musical. It has a hole in the bottom so I can walk."

"I see. You'll have trouble evading horny sailors."

"Yeah, well, Hans Christian Anderson was pre-MeToo."

This time, Tyler's smile is genuine. I can tell because it lands in the center of my chest like a blow.

I wish I could lick my suddenly dry lips without him taking credit for it.

He reaches into the car, and my breath hitches as he lifts his tie from around my neck, drawing it out in a long ribbon.

The silk strokes my neck for what feels like minutes, and I force my gaze away when he finally pockets the tie.

My attention lands on the lone motorcycle across the parking lot. "Next time Carly gets creative with my car, I'm borrowing your ride."

"No, you're not." He straightens, shoving a hand through his messy-is-sexy hair. "Jax

Jamieson would destroy me for letting his baby girl near it."

There it is. The reason I can't avoid Tyler completely, even I want nothing more than to cut him out of my life.

Oakwood's rebel prince doesn't live in a brick mansion with a closet full of V-necks and two Ivy-League-educated parents.

He lives in our pool house, thirty feet from my bedroom.

End of Sample

To continue reading, be sure to pick up *A Love Song for Liars* **at your favorite retailer.**

BOOKS BY PIPER LAWSON

FOR A FULL LIST PLEASE GO TO

PIPERLAWSONBOOKS.COM/BOOKS

OFF-LIMITS SERIES

Turns out the beautiful man from the club is my new professor... But he wasn't when he kissed me.

Off-Limits is a forbidden age gap college romance series. Find out what happens when the beautiful man from the club is Olivia's hot new professor.

WICKED SERIES

Rockstars don't chase college students. But Jax Jamieson never followed the rules.

Wicked is a new adult rock star series full of nerdy girls, hot rock stars, pet skunks, and ensemble casts you'll want to be friends with forever.

RIVALS SERIES

At seventeen, I offered Tyler Adams my home, my life, my heart. He stole them all.

Rivals is an angsty new adult series. Fans of forbidden romance, enemies to lovers, friends to lovers, and rock star romance will love these books.

ENEMIES SERIES

I sold my soul to a man I hate. Now, he owns me.

Enemies is an enthralling, explosive romance about an American DJ and a British billionaire. If you like wealthy, royal alpha males, enemies to lovers, travel or sexy romance, this series is for you!

TRAVESTY SERIES

My best friend's brother grew up. Hot.

Travesty is a steamy romance series following best friends who start a fashion label from NYC to LA. It contains best friends brother, second chances, enemies to lovers, opposites attract and friends to lovers stories. If you like sexy, sassy romances, you'll love this series.

PLAY SERIES

I know what I want. It's not Max Donovan. To hell with his money, his gaming empire, and his joystick.

Play is an addictive series of standalone romances with slow burn tension, delicious banter, office romance and unforgettable characters. If you like smart, quirky, steamy enemies-to-lovers, contemporary romance, you'll love Play.

MODERN ROMANCE SERIES

When your rich, handsome best friend asks you to be his fake girlfriend? Say no.

Modern Romance is a smart, sexy series of contemporary romances following a set of female friends running a relationship marketing company in NYC. If you enjoy hot guys who treat their families like gold, fun antics, dirty talk, real characters, steamy scenes, badass heroines and smart banter, you'll love the Modern Romance series.

ABOUT THE AUTHOR

Piper Lawson is a WSJ and USA Today bestselling author of smart and steamy romance.

She writes women who follow their dreams, best friends who know your dirty secrets and love you anyway, and complex heroes you'll fall hard for.

Piper lives in Canada with her tall and brilliant husband. She's a sucker for dark eyes, dark coffee, and dark chocolate.

For a complete reading list, visit www.piperlawsonbooks.com/books

Subscribe to Piper's VIP email list www.piperlawsonbooks.com/subscribe

amazon.com/author/piperlawson

bookbub.com/authors/piper-lawson

instagram.com/piperlawsonbooks

facebook.com/piperlawsonbooks

goodreads.com/piperlawson

THANK YOUS

First, thank YOU for picking up this book. I love that you trust me to entertain you. And I love entertaining you. It's such an EPIC win-win, I can't even.

This book wouldn't have happened without the support of my awesome advance team and reader group (ladies - thank you for the support, nail biting, and patiently rocking in the corner while I finished part this!). Extra shoutout to Beth and Tammy for doing an early read and holding my hand while I made final tweaks!

Natasha, thank you for the perfect cover. Lindee, I couldn't imagine better photography to inspire my books. You bring my characters to life!

Cassie and Devon of Joy Editing, thank you for

questioning, polishing, and catching all the little things.

Thank you Dani for getting the word out and making me a better doer AND planner! And Annette and Michelle... I would not be able to get these books to the people who matter most without your help. If there was an author life before your support, I was in a fugue state because I remember NOTHING.

Last but not least thank you Mr. L, the world's best beta reader and the guy who makes sure my world doesn't break while I'm sequestered in my writing cave.

Thank you all from the bottom of my heart. A little-known secret: the best part of author life isn't writing books. It's the privilege of having YOU ALL in my life.

Love. Always.

Piper

www.ingramcontent.com/pod-product-compliance
Lightning Source LLC
Chambersburg PA
CBHW030927210726

48290CB00007B/2099